JEDI QUEST

BY JUDE WATSON

THE SCHOOL OF FEAR

SCHOLASTIC INC.

New York   Toronto   London   Auckland   Sydney
Mexico City   New Delhi   Hong Kong   Buenos Aires

www.starwars.com
www.starwarskids.com
www.scholastic.com

ISBN 0-439-33921-9

Cover art by Alicia Buelow and David Mattingly.

12 11 10 9 8 7 6 5 4 3 2 1   3 4 5 6 7 8/0

Printed in the U.S.A.
First printing, February 2003

CHAPTER ONE

Patience was required of every Jedi. No matter what the pressure, a Jedi maintained inner calm. Every Padawan Learner knew the story of Jedi Master Yaddle, who had been imprisoned underground on Koba for several centuries and never lost her serenity.

Then again, Anakin Skywalker thought, *even Master Yaddle might have cracked if she had to deal with Senatorial procedure.*

Anakin hid his smile. Without seeming to move, he tensed and relaxed his muscles. He had been sitting for hours in the Polestar Reception Room off the Grand Hall of the vast Senate complex. The huge room had a soaring vaulted ceiling, which was gilded with sheets of precious metals from various worlds. The seating was low to the ground, wide with adjustable armrests for many-limbed beings. Plush cushions and reclining backs had tempted several beings into slumber. So did the large screens showing a droning speech in the main Senate chamber.

Anakin's Master, Obi-Wan Kenobi, sat quietly, every muscle still. His eyes rested on the gilded wall in front of him. To anyone walking by, he appeared completely composed. But Anakin knew his Master well, and he could sense an impatience that radiated like heat off Obi-Wan's stillness.

They had been sitting for most of the morning. Anakin could feel every minute of that wait in his coiled muscles. They had been summoned early that morning with the news that a decision on Obi-Wan's petition for an "order to reveal" had been reached. Obi-Wan had filed the petition against an influential Senator, Sano Sauro. When they'd arrived that morning, Obi-Wan had been directed by a Senatorial aide to wait "for just five minutes, please." That was three hours ago. They were still waiting.

Anakin's boot began to tap a quick rhythm on the stone floor. With one glance from Obi-Wan, Anakin stopped.

"Can I get you anything, Master? Tea?" Anakin asked. He would love to have something — *anything* — to do.

"No, thank you, Padawan. We will wait." Obi-Wan crossed his arms and resumed his intense scrutiny of the wall.

Nothing but the pursuit of Granta Omega would have brought them here. The galactic criminal had set his sights on the Jedi, and Obi-Wan had twice been his target. Omega was not practiced in the dark side of the Force, but he was fascinated with the Sith and knew that one was at large in the galaxy. He had set out to lure that Sith, and was willing to kill a Jedi in order to do so. He would amass even more wealth using any means he could. Obi-Wan considered him a great enemy of the Jedi.

Anakin had wanted to hunt him down, to start somewhere in the far-flung reaches of the galaxy and gather information, but Obi-Wan had counseled patience. They could wander the galaxy for months or years without getting any closer to Omega. Instead, Obi-Wan told Anakin, they must follow the only lead they had: Years before, Senator Sano Sauro had taken Omega on as his protégé, and was probably still in touch with him.

Sauro was also an enemy of the Jedi, though he cloaked it behind a silky manner and Senatorial procedure. Obi-Wan would have to force him to cooperate. In order to have access to the information Obi-Wan was sure was buried in his files, they would have to follow

Senate procedure. And Senate procedure was the one thing that Anakin knew his Master had no patience for. As a matter of fact, it was the one thing he knew that Obi-Wan was incredibly bad at.

So Obi-Wan had turned to an expert: a young Senate aide with a brilliant mind, the Svivreni Tyro Caladian. Tyro had made it his business to have at his fingertips the most unnecessarily complicated, ridiculously obscure, and surprisingly silly rules of order.

Tyro had explained that their only course of action would be to file an order to reveal. This order could be obtained only through a complicated series of steps that included petitions, signatures, approvals, and seals. Obi-Wan had made it through these steps, and at last the order had been served on Sano Sauro.

Anakin was sure that as soon as they gained access to Sauro's files, they would find the clue that would lead them to Omega.

Suddenly a Svivreni in a navy tunic burst into the vast room. His black hair flowed down his back, loosely held with a thick ring of dull metal. He was stocky and furred, his small, intense face screwed into an expression of nervous haste. He tried to modify his pace, but he ended up running and skidded to a stop before Obi-Wan and Anakin, his thin-soled boots sliding on the polished floor.

"I was tied up in a subcommittee hearing —" he said breathlessly.

Obi-Wan shook his head. "Doesn't matter. No news yet, Tyro."

Tyro Caladian shook his head rapidly. "How can that be? Something must be wrong."

Anakin frowned. He wasn't happy to hear Tyro say that.

"We had him in our grasp and he slipped away," Tyro moaned. "I can feel it."

"Nothing has happened yet," Obi-Wan said. "Have a seat before you fall down." A faint smile twitched at his mouth. Tyro's excitability amused the Jedi, but Tyro's vibrating nerves hid a political mind as sharp and cunning as a well-honed blade.

Tyro sat, sunk in gloom. He, too, was no fan of Sano Sauro. The Senator had attempted to take over the rich mines of Svivren for weapons development in a secret deal. The Svivreni were opposed to weaponry of any kind, and the deal was exposed before Sauro could complete his plan. He had covered his tracks well and they could not find proof to make an open accusation. It ate away at Tyro.

Tyro had worked together with Obi-Wan, making sure that they plugged every loophole. They had followed every item and sub-item of the procedure. They had notified, ratified, and petitioned. Obi-Wan had even enlisted the support of Supreme Chancellor Palpatine.

Despite Tyro's nerves, Anakin knew they'd prevail. He didn't understand why Tyro and Obi-Wan looked so worried.

Tyro blinked his small, bright eyes. "Sauro is pulling something. I wish I knew what it was."

Obi-Wan stirred. "I have a feeling we're about to find out."

Anakin quickly stood as the Speaker of the Senate, Mas Ameeda, strode into the room. He carried himself with his usual gravity, his hands clasped in front of him and his lethorns resting against the deep blue of his rich robes.

"Supreme Chancellor Palpatine has asked me to bring you this news," Mas Ameeda said after bowing to Obi-Wan. "Your order to reveal has been denied."

Anakin saw a flicker of anger in Obi-Wan's gaze, but it was gone in a moment. "On what grounds?"

"Senator Sauro has succeeded in utilizing a little-known procedural item called a sitting Senator's right of refusal," Mas Ameeda explained. "This has allowed him to block the order to reveal for an indefinite period. Senator Sauro is on an important committee on redistributing trade routes, and he petitioned the Senate Procedural Committee on that basis."

Tyro Caladian bristled. His fur stood out in sharp points. "I have never heard of a right of refusal," he said. "This is outrageous!"

Mas Ameeda stared at Tyro. It was clear he did not appreciate being lectured to by such a young aide. "It is a little-known rule, rarely used. The Committee had to go back three hundred years into the archives to find it."

"But procedural rules are discounted when they haven't been renewed and ratified within the last hundred years!" Tyro Caladian sputtered. "This is a clear violation!"

"It is a gray area," Mas Ameeda admitted. "Technically the Committee is in charge of interpreting all rules, so they have the right to enforce them. It is a . . . surprising decision." He turned to face Obi-Wan squarely. "Senator Sauro must have wanted to block your order very badly."

"I'm sure that is so," Obi-Wan said.

Mas Ameeda inclined his head. "The Supreme Chancellor wishes me to tell you that he did everything he could. He regrets the decision of the Committee but cannot overrule it. He hopes that you will be able to track Granta Omega some other way. He realizes that it is in the best interests of the galaxy for you to do so."

"Please extend my thanks to the Supreme Chancellor," Obi-Wan said.

Anakin could not believe his Master could keep his composure. To have come so close, and to be defeated by such a petty rule! It was unfair. How could his Master accept this ruling?

Mas Ameeda bowed gravely, then walked slowly out the door, his heavy robe swinging.

Tyro's fur was still raised, and his small eyes snapped with fury. "I'll fight this," he told Obi-Wan. "He won't get away with it. I'll draft an appeal."

"Do what you can, my friend," Obi-Wan said. "Yet I believe you will not succeed. My guess is that Sauro got to someone on that committee. I think that was what Mas Ameeda was insinuating." Obi-Wan put his hand on Tyro's shoulder. "Thank you for all your help. My Padawan and I will find another way."

Tyro looked crestfallen. "If ever you need me again, Master Kenobi, I am here for you." He raised a furred hand, fingers spread, in the Svivreni gesture of good-bye. Then he hurried from the room.

"Master, Tyro is right," Anakin said forcefully. "This is outrageous. Can't we break into Sauro's files?"

Obi-Wan folded his arms in the way that let Anakin know that he had gone too far.

"If we were discovered, it would undermine the Senators' trust in the Jedi," Obi-Wan said.

"There's got to be something we can do!" Anakin exploded. "We can't let him win. He's probably laughing at us right now!"

Obi-Wan gave him a severe look. "You should not be concerned with Senator Sauro's reaction. What does it matter if a corrupt man laughs at us? It should be less than the whisper of a gnatfly's wings to us."

Anakin stared at him. "He has made fools of us."

"No, Padawan," Obi-Wan said firmly. "If your path is the right one, no one has that power. Those who seek to make fools of others are fools themselves."

"I don't understand you," Anakin said, shaking his head. "You are just as upset as I am. I can feel it, Master. I know how much you want to find Granta Omega."

"Cultivate outward calm and inward calm will come," Obi-Wan said. "This is the time when the Jedi lesson of inner balance can help you. Accept the setback, and move on."

"How?" Anakin asked. "Where?"

"That is a question that is easy for me to answer," Obi-Wan said. "The Council has called on us for a new mission."

Anakin felt his anger drain away. "Do you know what it is?"

"No," Obi-Wan said. "But I will admit this — wherever it takes us, I will be glad to take a break from Senatorial politics."

CHAPTER TWO

To teach was easy. To be an example — well, that was another thing.

Obi-Wan had wanted to pound the floor and shake the very walls of the Senate. But with his Padawan by his side, he had too many reasons not to. He had drawn on his years of training in order to present a serene face to his apprentice. He knew Anakin struggled with his own patience. It would be damaging for Obi-Wan to show his frustration in front of him.

Anakin was sixteen years old. Impatience was wired into his being. Despite Anakin's strong Force connection, it would most likely take years before he developed true inner balance.

Obi-Wan, on the other hand, was supposed to have it already.

Obi-Wan drew a deep breath. It wasn't just the frustration of dealing with the Senate bureaucracy, blood-boiling as that was. It was the nagging feeling that if he didn't track down Granta Omega soon, their next meeting would be on Omega's terms. Obi-Wan didn't have anything concrete to go on. Yet he felt strongly that the darkness he felt around Omega somehow had to do with Anakin. The sense of urgency he felt was very real.

As they accessed the turbolift to the High Council tower, Ferus Olin walked up and nodded a greeting. As usual, the Jedi Padawan looked impeccable, his tunic spotless, his dark, gold-streaked hair drawn back severely in his Padawan braid. Even his utility belt gleamed from a recent polishing.

Obi-Wan turned to him, surprised. "You have been called as well?"

"Yes. My Master will join us in the High Council chamber."

They stepped onto the turbolift. Obi-Wan noted the cool nod Anakin gave in response to Ferus's greeting. So the two were still rivals. Perhaps being thrown together again would be good for both of them.

The three stepped out and entered the Council chamber. A majority of the Council was there, surrounding the trio in a semicircle. Outside the floor-to-ceiling windows dark clouds collided, threatening rain. A sudden bolt of lightning flashed a jagged streak of blue against the dark gray sky.

Mace Windu turned from where he'd been contemplating the coming storm. He sat in his chair and faced Obi-Wan, Anakin, and Ferus.

"Thank you for coming so quickly," he said. "This is a matter that demands our urgent response."

Obi-Wan waited, surprised that Mace Windu had begun without Siri's presence.

"There has been some infighting in the Senate," Mace Windu began.

Obi-Wan felt a silent groan well up within him. So much for his desire to escape Senatorial politics.

"Senator Berm Tarturi of Andara is fighting the political battle of his life," Mace continued. "The Andaran system is a thriving, influential one, but several planets in the system are claiming an imbalance in trade route distribution. The planet Ieria is demanding a new treaty, as well as representation in the Senate. Ieria and Andara have become bitter enemies. Senator Tarturi is concerned about a reduction in his own power, but the problem is bigger than that. Since the Andaran system is a powerful voting bloc, the Senate is worried about potential instability — as well as a full-scale civil war that could bring in other systems and spread throughout the Core Worlds. And something else has happened to complicate the situation even more. The Senator's son has disappeared."

Mace paused, knitting his long fingers together. "Gillam Tarturi is sixteen. He is a student at the elite Leadership School on Andara — a private academy that trains many of the children of the powerful throughout the galaxy for careers in government and diplomacy. The school's security system is sophisticated. The fact that Gillam disappeared without tripping any alarms is a mystery."

"Does Senator Tarturi believe that his son's disappearance is tied to his political problems in his home system?" Obi-Wan asked.

"He does," Mace Windu said. "He fears his opponents have kidnapped Gillam in order to distract him."

Obi-Wan sensed a hesitation in Windu's manner, and he quickly glanced at the rest of the Council members. It was always difficult to read them, but he felt the uncertainty in the air.

"Difficult the situation is," Yoda said. "Interested we are in another connection. A squad of young mercenaries there is."

"The word is that the Leadership School serves as a training ground for this squad," Windu continued. "The young mercenaries have already been involved in several intra-planetary disputes and possibly even assassinations. They are alleged to hire themselves out for various causes around the galaxy. The disappearance of Gillam Tarturi could be related to this secret squad. Their activities are beginning to worry the Council."

"So they must be investigated as well," Obi-Wan said.

Mace Windu nodded. "The Council has arranged for both Anakin and Ferus to enter the school as new students. They are to find out who is behind the renegade squad and investigate them. Their identities will be concealed — no one must connect the Jedi to this operation if we are to succeed. Not even the school officials will know that Ferus and Anakin are Jedi — they have been given documentation as transfer students, Anakin on a scholarship and Ferus as the son of a high official from a Mid-Rim planet."

"And meanwhile I will investigate Andaran system politics," Obi-Wan said. He tried to keep the thud of disappointment from his voice.

Mace Windu nodded again. "This will mean a separation between Master and Padawan. Not only for you, but for Siri as well. The Council is sending her to do some follow-up work on a planet in the Core. The Council feels that Ferus and Anakin together can handle this." He turned to the two Padawans. "You will be undercover at all times, and that will prove difficult in ways you have yet to foresee. You can set up a regular time to communicate with Obi-Wan. Students are not allowed to use comm devices during the school day, but they have a free hour in the evenings. You must check in with each other as often as you can."

"Yes, Master Windu," Ferus said.

The doors hissed open and Siri walked in with her usual purposeful stride. She bowed to the Council. "I have received my last instructions and I'm ready to leave," she said.

"You will be responsible for another Jedi's Padawan," Mace Windu told Obi-Wan. "You know what this means."

"It is as if he is my own," Obi-Wan said, looking at Siri. Her clear, deep blue gaze told him that she trusted him.

"May the Force be with you all," Mace Windu concluded.

An hour later, the sky remained black and the clouds still refused to release the rain as Obi-Wan stood on the landing platform with Anakin. Ferus was already in the cruiser, doing a last-minute check. Obi-Wan would remain on Coruscant to investigate Tarturi's rivals in the Senate. It was the place he had to start, but he did not relish the idea.

"I'm sorry to leave you, Master, but I know how much you're looking forward to returning to the Senate," Anakin said. The muscles around his mouth twitched as he tried not to smile.

"Very amusing," Obi-Wan said dryly. "I admit I would rather not have this particular assignment, but I recognize that it is necessary that it be done."

Anakin sighed. "Always an opportunity to teach."

"Yes," Obi-Wan said, smiling now. "That is the role of a Master, my young apprentice." He put his hand on Anakin's shoulder. "Remember, you are not on a solo mission. You are with a fellow Jedi. Do your best with Ferus. Try to get to know him. That might ease your irritation with him."

"I would rather not have this particular assignment, but I recognize that it must be done," Anakin said with a straight face.

Obi-Wan laughed. He would miss Anakin's humor. Sometimes, he knew, he could be too serious. He remembered how Qui-Gon would sometimes surprise him on a tough mission with a sly joke.

I must remember to do those things for Anakin, he thought. *His gifts are so great that I work too hard to teach. He must learn to enjoy, as well.*

"Keep in close contact, Anakin," he said. "I will be on Andara as soon as I can. May the Force be with you."

"May the Force be with you, Master." Anakin turned and strode toward the Republic cruiser. Obi-Wan felt a tug at his heart that he recognized as a reluctance he did not like to admit.

The Council believed that Anakin was ready for more independence, but no doubt they had chosen Ferus as a counterbalance. His stability would keep Anakin's impulsiveness in check.

Or so they believed.

Obi-Wan watched the cruiser shoot into a space-lane, suddenly reverse engines, and drop into a lane several levels below between an airspeeder and an air taxi with barely a millimeter to spare. Obi-Wan shook his head ruefully. There was no doubt in his mind that Anakin had suggested the close maneuver just to annoy Ferus.

He was glad Mace Windu had not seen it.

He watched the cruiser until it disappeared into the dusk. Yes, the Council was wise. Wiser than him. No doubt about that. Yet he knew his Padawan better than the Council, and his uneasiness gathered within him, as dark and heavy as the coming storm.

CHAPTER THREE

Andara was a beautiful world, lush and green with a temperate climate, tracts of wilderness, and wealthy cities. The Leadership School was on the outskirts of its capital city of Utare. The campus of the school took in rolling hills, green fields, and a lake. The grounds were ringed with an electro-charged security wall with observation towers and a particle shield. Roving surveillance droids made circuits of the property. Electro-bars covered the windows. Rich children usually attracted bounty hunters and other threats; the school meant to keep them out.

Anakin gazed behind him at the city buildings of Utare as they passed through the security checkpoint. He felt as though he were saying good-bye to freedom and entering a prison. Although there was security at the Temple, he never felt or saw its presence; he just felt safe.

Once they were inside the school and had received their class and room assignments, the feeling of oppression was meant to lift. The Leadership School was like a separate world. In many ways, it was more like a grand hotel than a place of learning.

It was built with gray stone imbedded with chunks of rare minerals that glinted blue and rose in the light. Costly woods were used for counters and desks. Each student had his or her own small but luxurious quarters. Expert chefs prepared the food. The students had extensive exercise equipment and five pools of varying depths and temperatures. Everything was arranged for their comfort. It was very different from the Temple. The Temple was both grand and simple at the same time. Here, luxury was everywhere.

"If the body is pampered, the mind is free to concentrate," Professor Aeradin told them as they toured the compound. He was an assistant dean and had been assigned to them for orientation. He was tall and thin, with a narrow head and four antennae that quivered when he grew excited. He was obviously proud of the school, and his antennae rarely stopped dancing.

But despite the teacher's enthusiasm and the gleaming hallways, Anakin felt a steady pulse underneath it all that leadened the atmosphere with dread.

"Can you feel it?" he asked Ferus as they made their way to their rooms.

Ferus nodded. "Fear."

Anakin said good-bye and opened the door to his small but exquisite suite. The sleep couch was piled with thick soft covers and a long counter held a variety of the latest tech learning devices.

All of the luxury was nice, he had to admit, but it made him uncomfortable. He liked simple things. And the luxury did not disguise the lack of freedom. The students were subject to strict security regulations. They could not leave the complex without authorization. The parents of the students paid a small fortune in order to ensure their children's safety. Security had been stepped up since Gillam's disappearance. Random checks were conducted and the whereabouts of the students had to be known at all times. Roving security droids zipped through the hallways, their cams constantly sweeping the air.

Yet Anakin knew these students did not feel safe here. The heavy surveillance didn't bother them. They welcomed it. Daughters and sons of privilege, they were used to constant attention. One of them had disappeared without warning. They all felt the chill of Gillam's absence.

He wasn't accustomed to keeping a low profile, but he tried to slip unnoticed through the halls as he went through the first few days of classes. He decided that his best strategy would be to cloak his abilities as much as possible. The more invisible he was, the more freedom he would have to examine others.

Slowly, he began to find it strange and liberating to be just another student. From the moment he had arrived at the Temple, he was whispered about. As the "Chosen One," the other students had kept an eye on his progress. Some were envious, some polite, some friendly, and some steered clear of him completely. But everyone noticed him. It was something that had been difficult for him in the beginning, but he had gotten used to it. Obi-Wan had told him that it was the best preparation for being a Jedi. He had to learn to screen out what others thought or speculated. He had to concentrate on his own path.

Around him were the elite leaders of tomorrow. They knew where they were going — on to positions of power in the galaxy, as Senators, rulers, heads of galactic corporations. Anakin marveled at their assurance, their expectation that their lives would be full of the same luxury and ease that had been theirs since childhood.

At night, alone in his room, he admitted a strange new feeling into his heart: envy.

Anakin sat in the Great Hall of Learning with the rest of the school. Although individual classes were small, once a week the entire school would gather for a General Information Contest. The students sat in rows underneath a gilded dome. Professor Aeradin stood on a repulsorlift platform, manipulating a holographic projector. The questions and problems were presented as holograms, and the students answered on datapads at their seats.

Like all of the desks and chairs at the school, these seats were plush and comfortable. Anakin could press a button and the seat configured to his body. It reclined and swiveled so that he did not have to move his head to follow the holographic problems.

He glanced at the problem overhead but waited a few seconds before entering his answer. There were many good things about Jedi training at the Temple, but Anakin discovered another one — any other school was easy compared to it. He had slipped into his classes with no problems. His training at the Temple had included classes in galactic politics, diplomacy, and extensive study of languages, system geography, and astronomy. He could follow his classes at the Leadership School with less than his full attention. Being at an elite school felt odd, but at least he could keep up academically.

A hologram of a system spun over his head, while planet after planet was highlighted with a bright blue light. As each world was highlighted, the native language or dialect repeated the same sentence.

Anakin did not need to wait until the question was complete. He already had figured out the Mid-Rim system. It was Rearqu 10.

"Name the system," Professor Aeradin said.

Anakin took his time entering his response. He watched the other students, noting who immediately entered an answer, who stared blankly at the system overhead, who tried to read what his neighbor had entered, and who whispered the answer to another. Then he entered his own.

Rearqu 10 flashed holographically overhead. The professor repeated it as the number of right and wrong answers appeared on a screen at the front of the room.

"Only forty percent were correct," Aeradin said severely. "Shameful."

The next problem flashed overhead. Anakin noted Ferus entering the answer before the question had even finished flashing. The student sitting next to Ferus glanced at him enviously, but Ferus's datapad was angled to prevent anyone from seeing what was on it.

Anakin sighed. Even undercover, Ferus had to be the perfect student.

Anakin entered his own answer. Across the room, a petite human girl with dark hair twisted in a thick knot at the nape of her neck smiled at him. He smiled back. She was in his Political Philosophies class and he had already noticed how bright she was. She had a way of seeing all sides of an issue and looking for the deeper meaning.

The contest wore on. At last the questions ceased. Professor Aeradin totaled up the responses on his data-pad and looked up.

"And the First Student today is . . ."

The name flashed holographically: FERUS OLIN

"I'd like to congratulate our new student, Ferus Olin, for his perfect score. His time was the best. Excellent work."

"Thank you, Professor Aeradin," Ferus said.

Suddenly another hologram rose next to Ferus's name. The light particles formed themselves into words, shining bigger and brighter: IS A SNOB

The auditorium exploded into laughter. Professor Aeradin looked up and saw the words. His gaze swept the auditorium while his antennae quivered with indignation.

"Who did this? Stand up this instant!"

The laughter slowly died, and the auditorium went still. Professor Aeradin's severe look traveled from student to student, trying to flush out the culprit.

Anakin drew on the Force to help him. He noted movement, whispers, a shift, a squirm. He felt the undercurrents in the room — suppressed laughter, nervousness. Impatience. Boredom. Hunger.

Triumph.

His gaze shifted to a short, scruffy human boy who sat staring innocently at Professor Aeradin.

The professor hesitated. "If I ever find out . . ."

His words were drowned out by a soft dinging. A voice rose from the hidden speakers. "End of contest. Five minutes to mod four. Five minutes."

"Dismissed," Professor Aeradin said helplessly, for the students had already risen, grabbing their datapads and talking and jostling as they surged toward the doors.

Anakin headed in the direction of the short boy. His sandy hair stuck up in bristles and it was easy to keep track of him. Anyone who could infiltrate a professor's holographic projector in order to conduct a practical joke might know something about bypassing security.

He noted that around him, students walked in groups or pairs. This boy walked alone.

"That was pretty wizard," Anakin said, falling into step beside the boy.

"What?" The boy shot him a surprised look from intelligent gray eyes.

"The hologram. You did it." Anakin waved a hand. "Don't worry, I won't tell. I'm impressed." He gave the boy a friendly grin. "Anakin Skywalker."

The boy hesitated. "Reymet Autem."

"So how did you do it?" Anakin asked.

"It's all in the wrist." Reymet mimicked entering items in a datapad and grinned. His gray eyes glinted. "Easy for a boy genius, my friend."

They headed down the hallway together. Anakin felt rather than saw Ferus fall in behind them.

Reymet waved a hand around him. "Welcome to the comfiest jail in the galaxy. It's not much, but we call it home."

"So how do you have fun around here?" Anakin asked.

Reymet shrugged. "I make my own fun."

The noise of the students anxiously hurrying toward lunch covered their words. "Must be hard, with all the security around here," Anakin remarked. He was pushing gently, trying to get Reymet to open up.

Reymet snorted. "Security isn't as secure as the experts say it is. There are ways to get around any system."

"It seems pretty tight to me," Anakin remarked casually.

Several students glanced at Anakin curiously as they passed by. Reymet shoved his datapad into his pocket with a rough gesture. "You'd better not be seen talking to me. Nobody talks to me."

"What about your friends?" Anakin asked.

Reymet scowled. "I don't have friends." He quickened his pace and disappeared into the crowd.

Ferus appeared next to Anakin. "Interesting."

"You heard?"

"Every word. I pick up something from him . . ."

"Me too. Not a darkness. Maybe just . . . confusion."

"He has something to hide," Ferus declared. "It could be anything, though. It isn't much of a clue."

"It's a place to start," Anakin said.

CHAPTER FOUR

The dining hall was a paneled room with soft, re-cessed lighting and thick red veda cloth hangings at the windows that muffled sound and cast a rosy glow on the diners. It was just like the exclusive restaurants Anakin had glimpsed on Coruscant — just like the spots the students were used to eating in, he was sure. And, like an exclusive restaurant, seating in the dining hall was subject to an unspoken code.

It hadn't taken Anakin long to realize that the best tables were by the windows and he was not welcome there. He didn't know why he felt a coolness from most of the students, but he definitely felt it. When he was looking for a seat at a table, an empty chair would be pushed aside to another table, or a datapad or a pile of durasheet notes would be quickly placed on the seat. It was clear that no one wanted to sit with him. There was a power elite in the school, and everyone else fell in around it.

Yet Ferus had been accepted almost immediately, and had his pick of places to sit. Was it because word had gotten out that he belonged to a powerful family on his homeworld?

You can travel to the ends of the galaxy and it will be the same — those with power do not like to share.

His Master had told him that once, in a voice of weary resignation. But sometimes Obi-Wan seemed to forget that Anakin had been a slave. If anyone knew about power, it was a slave. He knew about the hunger for it, and he knew about the humiliation of getting your nose rubbed in the fact that you didn't have it.

He took his bowl of aromatic stew to an empty table and sat. It wasn't that he needed company. Jedi were comfortable being alone. But inside, something burned, something deep and hot that he had hoped had been long forgotten. He took a bite of stew and tasted shame and anger. It was hard to swallow, like a mouthful of sand.

He reached inside the pocket of his tunic and withdrew a small, smooth stone. It was a river rock, a present from Obi-Wan. It had belonged to Qui-Gon.

The rock was Force-sensitive, but that was not why

Anakin reached for it during times of stress. When he rubbed his fingers along the smooth surface, it was as though he was able to draw on Qui-Gon's core of serenity. He thought of cool river water falling over his body, of turning his body like a fish and gliding in the deep green river, and his mind would go still. He and Ferus had to hide their lightsabers in their rooms, and the rock was the only physical connection to his real life.

A plate suddenly plunked down next to him. The same girl who had smiled at him in the General Information Contest pulled a stray chair over with her foot with the ease of an athlete. She sat down and sniffed appreciatively at her stew, then picked up her spoon. Anakin quickly slid the stone underneath the lip of his bowl, where it could not be seen.

"So, is this the enriching experience they promised you in the brochure?" the girl asked. "Students who are completely spooked snub you?" Her brown eyes twinkled at him. They were deep and warm and reminded him of another girl, more beautiful than this one — a queen, in fact. He saw the same intelligence, the same confidence. That memory more than the girl's friendliness, more than the river stone, dissolved the knot of anger in his belly.

The girl dug into her food with her spoon and swallowed an enormous bite. "Don't worry. It gets better."

"It does?"

She grinned. "You graduate." She stuck out her hand. "Marit Dice."

He shook it. "Anakin Skywalker."

"You're in my Political Philosophies class. You don't say much."

"You do."

She took another bite. "I have opinions," she said, shrugging. "The teachers think I'm too smart for my own good. Which doesn't matter much, because they don't matter. They won't give any scholarship student a good reference, anyway."

"Why not?" Anakin asked. Out of the corner of his eye, he saw Reymet leaning against a wall. Anakin noticed that Reymet was watching as Professor Aeradin forked up a large bite of lunch. Aeradin was supposed to be patrolling the dining hall, but he had filled up his plate from the buffet. Anakin had noticed that most teachers did this. He guessed that the students' food was much better than what was given to the teachers.

"Because they only give good references to the elite students," Marit said. She tore off a chunk of bread and dipped it in her bowl, then took a bite. "You should see what happens before graduation. The fathers and mothers and benefactors come, and they give the teachers presents. I mean, real presents. Like a landspeeder. Or tickets on a resort starship. Things like that. And suddenly their little darling winds up as a Senatorial aide." She waved the bread in the air.

Reymet suddenly reached for a custard tart and darted out of the room. Ferus signaled Anakin, then slipped out after Reymet.

Anakin would have liked to keep talking to this interesting girl, but he and Ferus had agreed to keep Reymet under surveillance. "That's too bad," Anakin said. "I think I need more tea. Will you excuse me for a minute?"

Marit shrugged again. "Sure."

Anakin hoped he hadn't been rude. He gave a quick glance to Professor Aeradin, still smacking his lips over his food, then slipped out the door. He saw Ferus at the end of the hallway and hurried up to him.

"Did you lose him?"

"He went into a restricted area," Ferus said. He pointed to a door that seemed closed until Anakin noticed that a tiny wedge had been placed between the edge of the door and the wall.

He leaned over to examine it. It was a small, flexible piece of transparisteel that was almost invisible. When he pushed on the edge, the door opened just enough for him to slip a hand inside. He reached around and felt for the controls. He pressed the button and the door slid open.

"Pretty clever," he said.

"It's the teacher's quad, so it's not alarmed," Ferus said. "I wonder what he's doing in there."

"Let's find out." Anakin hurried through the doorway. As soon as Ferus was through, he positioned the wedge and pressed the button to close the door. It slid almost shut.

"What if we get caught?" Ferus said. "We could get confined to our rooms between classes. How will we investigate?"

"Pretty simple. We'll have to avoid getting caught," Anakin said.

The hallway was empty. They proceeded, making no sound. Teachers' offices lined the walls, all of them unoccupied. The teachers were in class or monitoring the students. At the end of the hall was a door marked TEACHERS' LOUNGE. It was slightly ajar. Anakin put his eye against the crack.

Reymet had the custard tart between his teeth as he slipped a flat disk into a datapad and then placed it in a cabinet marked AERADIN. He closed the cabinet door and then punched several numbers into a pad at the side. Anakin heard a lock click.

Chewing, Reymet began to absently leaf through some durasheets left on the cabinet. Anakin eased back and motioned to Ferus.

"So that's how he infiltrated Professor Aeradin's hologram test," Anakin whispered. "He's pretty clever. He must have stolen Aeradin's disk when Aeradin was at lunch."

Ferus nodded. "He sure knows how to get around security measures. I think one of us should keep an eye on him. He's in two of my classes. I'll do it."

It was a logical conclusion, but Anakin still felt annoyed. Ferus hadn't really consulted him. It was more like he was thinking out loud. It was typical of Ferus's high-handed behavior, and yet he expected Anakin to cooperate with him without complaint. He knew if he told Obi-Wan this, his Master would brush aside his feelings and say that the mission was more important and that inner balance could not be attained without serenity.

This was all true, but Anakin would bet on one thing — when Obi-Wan was a Padawan, he didn't have to deal with anyone like Ferus Olin.

Anakin and Ferus hurried back to the dining hall. They knew that Reymet would be returning as well. Soon the midday meal would be over.

Students were beginning to gather their things and start for their classes as Anakin entered the dining hall and returned to his table. Marit was gone. He slid his fingers underneath his still-full bowl. So was his river stone.

CHAPTER FIVE

Obi-Wan was ushered immediately into Berm Tar-turi's private office. The Senator from Andara had a grand suite hung with delicate curtains of silver and gold shimmersilk. The different flowers of Andara were stitched with bright crimson thread into the fabric. Instead of a desk or table, Berm Tarturi sat on a platform with plush cushions. The platform had a work surface that swiveled up from underneath so that one could recline and work at the same time.

Tarturi was a large man with a bald head and a flowing black beard. He looked up at Obi-Wan, and the misery on his face was a contrast to the luxurious surroundings.

"I have heard from them at last." He pushed a datascreen toward Obi-Wan.

Obi-Wan walked forward to read it.

WE HAVE YOUR SON. WAIT FOR FURTHER INSTRUCTIONS.

On the screen was an image of a tall, muscular boy clutching a blanket around his shoulders. His mouth was twisted in a way that told Obi-Wan he was trying to be brave.

Obi-Wan felt his fury rise at the sight, but he kept his voice neutral. "Not much to go on," he said.

Berm dropped his head in his hands. "They are trying to torture me. There is a personal vendetta here. I can feel it."

"Do you suspect who it is?" Obi-Wan asked.

"It is Rana Halion," Berm said. "I'm sure of it. She's the driving force behind those who wish to overthrow the Andaran trade system. She's the ruler of Ieria, the next largest planet to Andara. I've known her for years. She's a ruthless politician. She has assembled a secret army and has persuaded several other worlds to join the effort. She is now at the Senate, lobbying for help for her cause. She claims the Andaran system needs two representatives in the Senate. She's trying to grab power, nothing more. She says she speaks for the majority of those in the Andaran system. It is a lie! *I* am the Senator of Andara. She will stop at nothing to get what she wants."

"She would kidnap a young boy?" Obi-Wan asked. "That is a serious charge, Senator."

He looked up at Obi-Wan bleakly. "She is a serious person. What are rules and laws to her? I'm positive that she or her supporters have broken into my office and looked through my files."

"Was security breached?" Obi-Wan asked.

"No, but I know she was here! Someone was!" Berm insisted. "I'm telling you, she has my son. What are you going to do about it?" Berm's voice had risen shrilly.

"I am here to find your son," Obi-Wan said calmly. "I will investigate what you have told me. Accusing her without proof would get us nowhere. And you don't want to endanger Gillam."

Berm slumped back against the cushions. "No, of course not. I haven't brought in Coruscant security because they are so heavy-handed. I knew the Jedi could handle this discreetly. It's just that I fear for Gillam. He thinks he is an adult. He is only sixteen." He glanced at the datascreen and his gaze softened.

"I know what that is like," Obi-Wan said, thinking of Anakin.

"We must find him soon," Berm said.

"Do you have enemies in the Senate?" Obi-Wan inquired.

Berm shook his head.

"I find that hard to believe, Senator," Obi-Wan said. "All politicians have enemies."

"Not me," Berm shot back. "Oh, I suppose I have political disagreements with my colleagues. But enemies? I do not cultivate them."

"We do not need to cultivate enemies," Obi-Wan said. "They flourish without us." He sensed that Berm Tarturi did not want to answer the question, so he tried a different tack. "Tell me about security at the Leadership School."

"I demanded a report from them that includes the data recorders from that night," Berm said. He reached over for a holofile. "Here is the report." He thrust it at Obi-Wan eagerly. "Perhaps you can find something in it. I couldn't. I had the best security experts go over it. I chose the Leadership School not only because of its reputation, but because of its security. It rivals the best in the galaxy. How could Gillam just disappear? That's what makes me think that Rana is responsible. She has a planetary treasury to draw on. She could hire the most sophisticated tech team in the galaxy to override the system. Didn't she break in here without tripping the alarm?"

Obi-Wan took a quick look at the holofile in his hands. "Everything seems in order, but I'll have the analysts at the Temple go over this. How often do you communicate with your son normally?"

"Almost every night. The school has a contact hour in the evenings. Otherwise he is on comm silence."

Obi-Wan knew this. Students were restricted in use of communication devices except for a one-hour period. It was the time he had set up to speak with Anakin and Ferus.

"We're very close," Berm went on. "His mother died three years ago."

Obi-Wan looked down at the security report. "It says here that you last checked in with Gillam over a month ago."

Berm flushed. "There are many details at the Senate that require my attention. That doesn't mean I'm not close to my son."

"Did Gillam have special friends at the school?"

"Of course. He's very popular."

"What are their names?"

Berm looked at him blankly. "Ah . . . let me see. Hmm. I don't recall. The stress of this whole affair has been so great, it's hard to remember every detail. . . ."

"How about vacations? Where did Gillam spend his?"

"With me, of course. Unless my duties here prevented him from joining me. Then he would spend vacations at our mountain home on Andara."

"By himself?"

"Of course not. There were servants in attendance."

Obi-Wan nodded. He was beginning to get the picture of a lonely boy.

Berm seemed to sense this, for he said quickly, "But he loved coming here to visit me. He was just here a month ago. He wants to be a Senator, like me. We are very close."

"Of course," Obi-Wan said. "Let me take this message with me, and I'll keep you updated."

"Anything I can do for my son, I will do," Berm said.

"I appreciate that, Senator Tarturi," Obi-Wan replied. He believed that the Senator was sincere. But he did *not* believe that Tarturi had told him everything. Senators were used to concealing some of the truth in order to place themselves in the best light. It was their nature. He needed a clear view of Senator Tarturi's role in the Senate, and he knew just who to ask.

Obi-Wan tried to access the door to Tyro Caladian's tiny office, but the door stuck after it had slid open only a few centimeters.

"Tyro?" he shouted inside the crack.

"Go away," a muffled voice answered.

"It's Obi-Wan!"

"Obi-Wan! For star's sake, don't move." Obi-Wan

heard the sound of crashing and banging. "I'm coming —
oof! Don't . . . I'm almost there . . . ah!"

The door slowly opened, pushed by Tyro. "Can't
you . . ." he puffed ". . . use your Force . . . to help?"

Obi-Wan leaned against the door frame, watching.
"I'm enjoying this too much."

Tyro got the door all the way open. He wiped his
forehead, where his fur had matted with sweat. "So
happy to amuse. Thanks."

Obi-Wan strolled inside. Tyro's office was filled with
plastoid boxes crammed with durasheet documents.
More plastoid file boxes were stacked against a wall.
Some of the boxes had been shoved against the door,
causing it to jam. "What's going on?"

"I told you I'd get something on Sano Sauro," Tyro
said, climbing over a box to get to a holodocument-
strewn desk. "I requisitioned all the documents in the
Senate registry that involve his homeworld. He couldn't
seal everything, just his personal docs."

"All of them?" Obi-Wan asked incredulously. "But
he's been a Senator for nine years!"

Tyro ruefully surveyed the crowded office. "Well, it
might take a while. But what can I do for you, Obi-Wan?
I'm at your service, as always."

"What do you know about Berm Tarturi?" Obi-Wan

asked. He raised a hand and used the Force to push aside a tower of documents in order to sit down.

Tyro looked from the ease of Obi-Wan's gesture back to the door he had struggled with. His ears twitched as he sat down. "I sure could use that Force of yours. Think how I could save on maid service. Anyway — Tarturi. The one whose son has been kidnapped."

Obi-Wan was startled. "How do you know that? There's been no official word."

Tyro smiled, his small, pointed teeth glistening. "Why are you in this office?"

Obi-Wan inclined his head. "Because you hear everything."

"What exactly do you need to know?" Tyro said. "I know many things about Senator Tarturi. For example, at the moment he is engaged in the fight of his political career."

"Who is his biggest enemy in the Senate?" Obi-Wan asked.

"Are you serious?" Tyro said. "You don't know?"

"Why else would I be here?" Obi-Wan asked irritably. "Because I enjoy filing?"

"*Sano Sauro* is his biggest enemy," Tyro said.

"Sauro?" Obi-Wan felt his pulse quicken. "Tarturi didn't mention him."

Tyro snorted. "He wouldn't. They are locked in a bitter battle over the redistribution of trade routes. Typical Senate bureaucratic tangle, but for them — it might as well be life or death. It means money, payoffs . . . and reelection. The battle has left them mortal enemies."

"But why wouldn't Tarturi tell me this?" Obi-Wan wondered.

"Because Senators never admit they have enemies, Obi-Wan," Tyro said patiently. "Don't you know that by now? It gives their opponents more power if they acknowledge them."

"Even when his son is missing?"

Tyro laughed, but the laugh had no humor in it. "His mother could be missing, his wife, and his pet nek battle dog. He still wouldn't tell you everything."

"So," Obi-Wan said thoughtfully, "if Berm Tarturi was distracted by his son's kidnapping . . ."

"Sauro could profit handsomely," Tyro finished. "The committee is in session right now. If Tarturi misses even one meeting, Sauro could gain the upper hand." Tyro sat up straighter. "Do you think Sauro could be involved?"

"Does Sauro know Rana Halion?" Obi-Wan asked.

"The leader of the Andaran opposition? I don't think so," Tyro answered. "But if he did meet with her, it would have to be in secret. Naturally he would support her efforts in the Andaran system. It would destroy Tarturi's power base." Tyro tapped a triple-jointed finger on a pile of datasheets. "Not to mention that Halion could get her new trade routes if she throws her support to Sauro. They both have much to gain from an alliance."

"So if Halion cooked up a plot to kidnap Gillam Tarturi, Sauro might help," Obi-Wan said.

Tyro nodded. "My enemy's enemy is my friend, you mean."

"Or he could have cooked up the plot and enlisted her. It is certainly something he is capable of."

Tyro's ears twitched excitedly. "If we could find proof, it would mean the end of his career. I'd have him in prison. And you'd have your files. The block of the order to reveal would be dissolved."

"And we'd find Gillam Tarturi," Obi-Wan said.

CHAPTER SIX

"Today we shall consider the geopolitical effect of the great Lali Plague," Professor Win Totem said. Then she sat down with great dignity, right on a custard turnover.

The class exploded with laughter. It went on a little too long, Anakin noted. The constant anxiety the students felt led them to grasp at any relief.

The tall professor with the regal bearing stood and regarded the ruby-colored stain on the back of her white septsilk gown.

"Ferus Olin," she rapped out. "You are responsible for this!"

Ferus started. "I assure you, Professor, I am not."

"Ten more demerits for lying," Professor Win Totem barked. Her blue skin flushed an angry purple. "You are the only one who could have done it. I asked you to distribute the notes before class."

Anakin watched as Ferus clenched his hands. He knew what Ferus was thinking. Ferus and Reymet had distributed the notes together. They did everything together now. Flattered by Ferus's attention, Reymet had become his tagalong. But Reymet couldn't resist playing his practical jokes, and Ferus was getting blamed. Anakin also knew that Ferus could not point the finger at Reymet. He was trying to befriend him. Besides, if Ferus told on Reymet, he'd be a tattletale, what the students called a womp fink.

Reymet's face was pure innocence. He shook his head with concern as he studied the stain on Professor Totem's gown.

Totem turned back to the lesson. Anakin hid his grin as he bent over his datascreen. It served Ferus right. He had grabbed the assignment to watch Reymet. He deserved the consequences. Anakin couldn't imagine two people more unlike each other than Ferus and Reymet. He knew that the secret pleasure he got from watching Ferus being blamed for a practical joke wasn't very Jedi-like, but on the other hand, he couldn't wait to tell his friends Tru and Darra that Ferus had gotten demerits for putting a custard turnover on a teacher's chair.

Out of the corner of his vision, he saw Marit eyeing him curiously. He had been playing a waiting game with her. After he'd discovered that his stone was missing, his first impulse was to rush after her and demand it back. It was his most precious possession, and he hated being without it.

But he had stopped himself. What would Obi-Wan have done?

Take a breath and think, Anakin.

So he asked himself why Marit had taken it. She must have known that he would immediately realize that she had it. Did she want to provoke a confrontation? Did she want to see what he would do?

Anakin had decided to wait. Not the easiest course of action for him. Not at all. But he was puzzled and intrigued by Marit, and he wanted her to feel the same. Let Ferus chase after Reymet. Anakin's instincts told him that there was more to Marit than he knew.

So even though he felt her eyes on him, he didn't turn. Nor did he acknowledge her when Professor Totem had them break into groups and Marit joined his. He didn't respond when she tried to catch his eye, even during the most boring stretch of the professor's lecture.

She would come to him, he knew. After the class, she would find a pretext to talk to him. He was driving her crazy because he had waited her out.

Better to wait to catch your prey than strike too soon.

Obi-Wan had counseled him again and again on the virtue of patience. At last he was beginning to under-stand why his Master pushed it. It worked. Sometimes.

The class ended. Anakin headed out the wide carved door. He left the hallway and accessed the brushed durasteel doors that led to the courtyard. Even though it was overlooked by windows, it felt removed. It was a gloomy, dark day, and he had it to himself. Students avoided isolated places now. They traveled in pairs or groups and went directly to their classes.

"All right, I give up the battle," Marit said from be-hind him.

He turned. "I didn't know we were in a war."

She held up the stone. "You know I have this. Don't you want it back?"

"Yes," Anakin said. Even in the gloom, the river stone shone, its shiny black surface like a mirror full of reflected light.

"And you didn't report me."

"No."

"This stone is important to you. I can tell. Why?"

"It was a gift," Anakin said.

"From your father?"

Longing burst inside him. He did not have a father. Shmi had been very clear about that. He didn't understand it, but he accepted it. He did not think about his lack; he never had. But unexpectedly the ache would well up in him and take him by surprise.

Then he thought of Obi-Wan, and the ache went away.

"Yes," he said. "Are you going to give it back?"

She held it up, fingering it thoughtfully. "I'm not sure yet."

It would be so easy for him to use the Force to get it back. Instead, Anakin moved. His kick barely grazed her fingertips, but it dislodged the stone and sent it flying straight toward him. He reached up with one hand and caught it.

Marit blinked. She looked down at her hand, still outstretched but now empty. "I didn't even see you move. How did you do that?"

Anakin slid the stone back into the concealed inside pocket of his tunic. "Lots of practice. Now it's your turn to answer questions. Why did you take it?"

Her dark eyes glinted. "Because I wanted to see what you would do."

"A test," Anakin said. "Did I pass?"

Marit only smiled and changed the subject. "I saw you in the flight simulator the other day. You were pretty good."

It was the one area where he had not hidden his

skill. It was hard for Anakin to sit in a cockpit and not fly fast and expertly. "Thanks."

"I'd like you to meet some friends of mine. Will you come with me now? It's our free mod."

Anakin nodded. Marit may not have answered his question about passing her test, but she didn't need to. He had passed. The question was, for what purpose?

CHAPTER SEVEN

Obi-Wan stared down at the holofile in front of him. He flipped through the data for what felt like the thousandth time. He couldn't find the key.

Something had happened the night Gillam disappeared, yet the security record showed that nothing had been breached. Obi-Wan had gone over the report. The best security expert at the Temple, Jedi Knight Alam Syk, had gone over it. Nothing was out of the ordinary. It was as though Gillam had disappeared into thin air.

Obi-Wan had also gone over the short note sent by the kidnappers. It was strange that they had not asked for credits or made any demands. The note seemed more like a delaying tactic than anything else. There was a chance the note could be linked to a particular datapad, but until they had a suspect, they could do nothing with it.

Obi-Wan looked at the security report again. He had the nagging feeling that he was missing something obvious.

His comlink signaled, and he answered it brusquely. "Yes?"

Tyro's excited voice vibrated through the air. "I've got something. I analyzed the data from the past five years of Sauro's illicit activity — the stuff he's been caught at, anyway — and ran it through my probabilities program, looking for connections. I narrowed his secret meeting places to three. Then I cross-referenced his schedule and committee meetings, and —"

"Tyro," Obi-Wan said with great patience, "please, get to the point."

"He's meeting Rana Halion secretly," Tyro said in a rush.

"Now?"

"I think so. I'm following her right now, and she's heading to a place he's used for secret meetings in the past. It's just a hunch, but —"

"Tell me where," Obi-Wan demanded.

Tyro gave him the directions. Obi-Wan rushed out of the Temple. He took one of the Temple's speeders and raced through the jammed space lanes of Coruscant, diving several hundred levels below to a grassy quad surrounded by stores and cafés. He parked the speeder and quickly hurried to the prearranged spot where Tyro was waiting.

Tyro sat in a crowded café under an awning that cast deep shade. From here he had a view of the quad seating. With a nod at Tyro, Obi-Wan sat next to him and surveyed the area.

It was a wise choice of location for a secret meeting, he thought. The many stores and cafés made for crowded passageways. There were numerous entrances and exits, and several busy space lanes converged nearby. Glass turbolifts connected to levels above and below. If someone needed to get lost quickly, it would be easy to do.

"There she is," Tyro said in a low tone. "Right on schedule."

Obi-Wan looked curiously at Rana Halion. He had studied her image in her docs, but she appeared more commanding in person. Dressed to blend with the crowd, she was wearing a brown traveler's cloak with a hood. She was a tall, lanky humanoid with white hair cut short and twisted into spikes. Wide gold cuffs encircled each strong wrist. Even from this distance, he noted the intensity of her eyes, a blue so light they were almost colorless.

She strolled around the quad, glancing in shop windows. To a casual passerby, she appeared to be window-shopping. But Obi-Wan saw how her glance continually darted to the seats on the quad. She was definitely waiting for someone.

Tyro ordered a round of drinks so that they wouldn't be conspicuous. Obi-Wan sipped his juice, alert for any sign of Sano Sauro. The minutes ticked by.

He could see the impatience in Rana Halion's walk. Her hands twisted together, then relaxed. She sat for several minutes, then got up to stroll again.

"Where is he?" Obi-Wan asked.

"I don't know," Tyro fretted. "I'm certain he's meeting her. It's too much of a coincidence, her being in this place. You'd think if you go to all the trouble of putting someone under surveillance that they would cooperate. How can Sauro do this to us? It's like he knows we're here."

Obi-Wan suppressed a groan. He held out his hand. "Let me see your comlink."

Tyro handed it to him. "What is it?"

Obi-Wan took out his own comlink and contacted Alam Syk at the Temple. "Can you run a trace on this?" he asked, reading off the data from Tyro's comlink.

Within seconds, Alam answered, "It's got a trace on it. Coming from . . . the Senate. Hang on . . ." Obi-Wan heard data keys clicking. Alam could trace any signal. "Hmmm. Do you know a Senator Sano Sauro? It looks like he's interested in what Tyro Caladian is up to."

Obi-Wan tossed the comlink back to Tyro. "There's your answer. I suggest that you do a routine sweep of your comlink transmission security in the future."

"I was never important enough before to need to do so," Tyro said. "I guess that's a good sign."

"Except that we lost our chance to trap Sauro," Obi-Wan said.

Across the quad, a disgusted Rana Halion strode off and hailed an air taxi.

"What next?" Tyro asked. "I doubt Sauro will use any of the usual places again."

"Which is why it's time to confront him directly," Obi-Wan said. "Time is running out for Gillam."

Sano Sauro was at a Senate function attended by many dignitaries. Obi-Wan and Tyro slipped easily into the crowd. Obi-Wan spotted Sano Sauro and made his way over to listen. Tyro joined a group surrounding Berm Tarturi.

"So glad you could join us after all," a Senator was saying to Sauro. "The commemoration of the dedication of the plaque on the south-facing wall of the main north-south corridor of the northeast wing of Complex B is an important step forward in promoting the harmony of the galaxy."

"I agree," Sauro said smoothly. "Another plaque with a quotation concerning the necessity for peace will certainly heal the many bloody, savage conflicts."

The other Senator proudly puffed out his scaly green cheeks. "The artisans of my home system were responsible for the plaque."

"Then I am doubly sure it will do its job," Sauro answered. There was no trace of irony in his tone, Obi-Wan noted, but Sauro managed to convey it. Yet the apparent sincerity of his tone would make it difficult to challenge him. So did his impassive expression. The skin was stretched so tightly over the bones of his face that he rarely registered an emotion.

He caught sight of Obi-Wan. "Will you excuse me?"

Sauro suddenly headed for the exit, slithering through the crowd with the expertise of one used to escaping dull gatherings. Obi-Wan started after him, but suddenly Berm Tarturi's voice boomed out. Sauro stopped abruptly but did not turn.

"How kind of you to say that," Berm said to the group of Senators surrounding him. "No, I'm trying to keep it very quiet. It is a private matter. Yet others seek to exploit my sorrow. Oh, it's not that I expect special treatment, but those who would take advantage of a father's despair . . ." Tyro raised his eyebrows at Obi-Wan. Obviously, Tarturi abandoned discretion when he could gain sympathy.

Obi-Wan saw Sauro's sneer. He was contemptuous of Tarturi's tactics.

Sauro turned. His voice, hard as ice, cut through Berm's blustering like a laser. "Yes, anyone who exploits private pain is despicable." He gave Tarturi a withering look. "No matter who does it."

The Senators looked back and forth between the two enemies, some with apprehension, others avidly looking forward to a war of words. Tyro's eyes gleamed, no doubt hoping Sauro would let something slip in anger. But Sauro simply turned his back on Tarturi and slipped off through the crowd, a slim figure in black.

A group of Senators suddenly converged on Berm Tarturi while others faded back, and it took Obi-Wan several precious seconds to extricate himself from the crowd. When he pushed his way out the door, Sauro had already disappeared. Obi-Wan headed toward Sauro's suite of offices.

As soon as he entered, Sauro's personal assistant stood up. "He isn't here."

"Did he tell you to say that?" Obi-Wan brushed past him, heading for the door.

"I am calling security."

"Your choice." Obi-Wan had no more patience for protocol. He waved a hand and used the Force to slide open the door to Sauro's inner office.

Sauro turned, startled, as Obi-Wan strode in. "This is outrageous!" he sputtered, losing his usual cool.

"You are meeting with Rana Halion secretly," Obi-Wan said.

"You don't have any evidence of that," Sauro said, regaining his composure.

"I have evidence that you put Tyro Caladian under surveillance," Obi-Wan continued.

Sauro stood behind his long desk. He was not a tall man, but the desk was low to the ground in order to give that impression. The tall red thorns of the claing bush rose from the corners, stabbing the air. His thin lips twisted as he leaned forward, resting on his knuckles. "And why shouldn't I? I don't take kindly to being investigated by young upstart attorneys. I have a legitimate concern as to who exactly this Caladian is and what he wants. The risk of assassination and sabotage are part of this job, and I must take any steps I can to protect myself. If you wish to take it up with the Senate security committee, do so."

"You rely on those committees," Obi-Wan said. "No doubt because you have bribed your way onto most of them."

"What is this personal vendetta you have against me, Kenobi?" Sauro's voice purred now. "I must confess, I don't understand it. I've done nothing to antagonize you. Perhaps I should bring you up on charges."

"What charges?"

"Breaking and entering, for one," Sauro said, his gaunt face expressionless. "The Force is a weapon like any other."

"The Force is not a weapon," Obi-Wan snapped. "Let me warn you, Sauro. I am investigating Gillam Tarturi's kidnapping. If I find you had anything to do with it —"

Sauro laughed. "A child's kidnapping! Hardly something I would dabble in. You are grasping at straws, Kenobi. And once again you are wasting my time." He picked up his comlink and stabbed at a button with his index finger. "I think I will report you for harassment. Perhaps a few hours of being detained by Senate security will help you calm down."

"Your threats reveal your fear," Obi-Wan said. "I'll be back."

CHAPTER EIGHT

Marit's friends sat together on the athletic field outside. They seemed to be expecting Anakin. He noted one friend looking him over carefully, from the top of his head to his boots. The student, a Bothan, stood as soon as they came up.

"So this is the one," he said. He was short, shorter than Marit, and the curling hair down to his shoulders gave him a soft look that was undercut by his shrewd gaze. This was clearly not someone to underestimate.

"This is Anakin," Marit said. "Anakin, meet Rolai Frac. And this is Tulah, and Hurana, and Ze."

"Have you ever ridden a swoop?" Ze asked. He was a humanoid, short and plump, with close-set green eyes and two pigtails that hung down his back. He seemed eager for action.

"A couple of times," Anakin said.

"We were going to have a swoop race," Tulah said. Anakin recognized the elongated head and pale skin of a native of Muunilinst. Tulah was tall and skinny, with a shock of bright yellow hair that stuck straight up from his head. His voice was all business. "Do you want to join us?"

"Just once around the school grounds," Marit said.

"Sounds like fun," Anakin said.

"The only thing is, it's technically against the rules," Hurana said. She gave him a shy smile, but he could tell he was being tested. "You're going to have to avoid the roving surveillance droids."

"Sounds even better," Anakin said.

Marit pointed to a nearby swoop with her chin. "That's yours, then. Watch out for professors and security cameras. Let's go."

Marit and her friends slung their legs over their swoops. Anakin followed. He took a moment to get used to the swoop controls and was a few seconds behind them. He wasn't worried. He knew how to fly a swoop faster than anyone.

He took off after them, streaking across the gray sky. Ahead was a security checkpoint. Anakin could see the camera lenses revolving. Marit gunned her motor and flipped her swoop sideways to avoid being tracked.

A second later, Hurana dipped below it, missing it by only a fraction. Anakin saw her grin and knew she had timed it that way. The others followed expertly.

Anakin was impressed. He increased his speed, timing his approach with the revolving camera lenses. He pulled the swoop up and then down quickly, missing the lens by a comfortable half second.

He pushed the engine to maximum and quickly caught up to the others. He didn't slow down but zoomed by them. He saw Rolai's surprised face, but Marit looked worried.

He saw why. Below him a group of professors had paused on the stairs outside one of the academic buildings, talking. Any moment they would see him.

He turned the swoop to the left and headed for the dense branches of an enormous tree. Behind him, he saw Marit pull her swoop up and circle out of range of the professors.

Anakin could hover in the branches, but he was too impatient. He dipped below one branch and zoomed up to skim above another. He snaked in and out of the thick branches, leaning his body first one way, then the other. He did not make even one leaf tremble. The professors continued to talk, completely unaware of the swoop above them.

The others skirted the trees, looping around to

avoid the professors and adding crucial minutes to their times.

He cleared the grove of trees out of sight of the professors, as well as Marit and her friends. A surveillance droid revolved ahead, surprising him for only an instant. Anakin pulled the swoop to a hard right, avoiding the rotating sensors. Then he dove beneath the droid and zoomed on.

Grinning, Anakin leaned over the handlebars and gunned the motor. He skirted a security camera and dove beneath a tractor beam. This was child's play for him.

The others were in sight again but still well behind him as he cleared a rooftop and did a quick triple loop dive to avoid being seen by a class of students playing laserball below. Then he dropped from the sky and landed in the same precise spot he had left from. He sat down and crossed his legs in a leisurely fashion.

A short two minutes later, Marit and the others pulled up. Anakin was surprised at their speed. They were almost as fast as a Jedi on a swoop. Marit swung off her swoop and strode toward him, tossing her braid behind her shoulder.

"Okay, hotshot," she said. "You win."

"What do I win?" Anakin asked. "If it's the chance to break out of here," he joked, "count me in." He spoke lightly, but he could feel how close he was to being accepted. He didn't need the Force to pick up on the humming energy among the group of friends. Something was definitely up. Had he found the secret squad the Jedi High Council spoke of?

"You see?" Marit said to Rolai. "I told you he could fly."

"He can fly," Rolai agreed.

"He's almost as good as me," Hurana said. Her pale gold eyes held a new respect.

"We have a sort of club," Marit said. "Not a school club. A serious club. Are you interested?"

"I'm not sure yet," Anakin said. "Why don't you tell me about it?"

"We take on assignments from outsiders. Beings who need a little help. We use our skills to aid them. If my friends and I have one thing in common, we don't like to see others get kicked around. I think you're that way, too."

"I am," Anakin said. "What exactly do you do? Rescue fluffkits from trees?"

Rolai looked annoyed. "This isn't a joke. Two weeks ago on Tierell, we changed the course of a planet's history."

"And made a bundle of credits," Tulah said. "Don't forget that."

"We do whatever is needed," Marit said quickly. She gave Rolai a warning glance, as if he'd said too much. "You'll learn more if you join us. Look, I told you how it works here. They only run the scholarship program so that they'll look good. They don't care about us. They won't help us. No one will. We have to help ourselves. Why should we wait around to get passed over for good jobs when we can start our lives now?"

"I agree," Anakin said. "But how do you get off campus? You'd have to violate security."

Marit shook her head. "We're able to conduct the missions on our free days. We have permission to leave. We just have to be sure to be back in time. And there are ways to trick security." She grinned at Rolai. "Rolai is our security expert and financial officer. Ze handles communications."

Ze nodded. "Comlinks, datapads, holo transmissions. Traces and countertraces. There are plenty of frequencies to hide in, if you know how."

Anakin was impressed. Even he didn't know how to navigate the complicated process of concealing a transmission origin.

"I'm transportation," Hurana said. "I get us in and out, and fast."

Tulah lifted a finger. "I'm battle strategy. But mostly I'm comic relief."

Tulah spoke lightly, but something in his face told Anakin that his joking was a pose to hide a serious purpose.

"And I research the proposals," Marit said. "I'm the galactic politics expert."

"So what am I?" Anakin asked.

"We need someone who knows something about sophisticated air transport like starfighters," Hurana said. "I know some, but Marit has been watching you, and she says you know more."

"I don't know about that," Anakin said. "But I did grow up fixing engines. So how do you decide what you're going to do?"

"We consider proposals and vote on them," Hurana said. "Everyone's vote is equal."

"And every decision is unanimous," Tulah said. "If one of us doesn't want to take an assignment, we pass on it. You'd get an equal vote, too, fly-guy. Just try to vote with me."

Unlike the others, Rolai's look was cool. Anakin had the feeling that he would have to prove himself to the Bothan before he welcomed him. It didn't bother him. He might feel that way himself with an outsider.

"The kind of assignments we take on are important," Marit said. "We're just starting, but already what we can do has spread to the right beings. We're on the side of justice in the galaxy. The powerful exploit the weak. We try to tip the balance. In one of our last missions we broke into the records of a company that was dumping its toxic garbage on a neighboring planet's moon. We exposed them and got paid for it. We can get away with a lot because adults tend not to notice kids. They underestimate us."

Rolai grinned. "Big mistake."

To his surprise, Anakin found himself liking what he was hearing. It was almost like being a Jedi, but without Masters. No one told the squad what to do. They picked their own missions and were responsible only to themselves.

"Count me in," he said.

CHAPTER NINE

Anakin met Ferus at their prearranged spot in the computer lab during their free time before lights out. Most of the students were in their own rooms, studying or talking. No one liked to venture out into the halls at night, no matter how good security was now. The computer lab was open but empty. They spoke in low voices in a corner.

"Reymet keeps dropping hints," Ferus said without waiting for Anakin to speak. "He says he knows something about some secret goings-on at the school. He even has hinted that it has something to do with Gillam's disappearance. I know he's trying to impress me, but I still think he knows something. Maybe about the secret squad. If we could infiltrate it, we'd finally have something to tell Obi-Wan."

"I *did* infiltrate it," Anakin said.

Ferus looked startled. "Why didn't you tell me?"

"You didn't give me a chance," Anakin said. As usual, Ferus got under his skin. "It just happened today."

"How? Who is it? This is great news," Ferus said approvingly.

Anakin wasn't sure what annoyed him more — Ferus's lack of envy at his progress, or the way his approval sounded just a bit condescending, as though Ferus was his Master.

"I was approached by Marit Dice," Anakin said. "She and her friends are all scholarship students here at the school. That's the key. They feel that they won't be treated fairly when it comes to positions after graduation, so they decided to strike out on their own. The school doesn't help them. They only help the sons and daughters of the important people."

"Sounds like an excuse to me," Ferus said.

"No," Anakin said, annoyed. "I'm sure it's true. Haven't you noticed that the other students don't talk to the scholarship students?"

"Not really," Ferus said. "After all, I talk to Reymet."

"Only because you have to."

Ferus sighed. "So they picked you because you're a scholarship student."

"They picked me because they thought they could trust me," Anakin said. "I don't have a reputation as a snob."

If Ferus felt the sting of Anakin's remark, he didn't show it. "Did they say anything about Gillam? Do you know if he was in the squad?"

"They didn't say a word about Gillam," Anakin said.

"That's strange," Ferus said. "It's all everyone else at school talks about."

"They have more important things on their minds," Anakin said.

"Is Marit the leader?"

Anakin gave this some thought. "She did most of the talking. But I didn't get the feeling that she was the leader. They say they vote on everything."

"Do you know if they're going out on an assignment?" Ferus asked.

Anakin shook his head. "Not yet. I'll find out."

Ferus frowned. "So do you think there's a connection? And if there is, what could it be?"

"I don't know," Anakin said. "I can't imagine them kidnapping a fellow student. They seem straightforward. They take on good causes. They're almost like Jedi, in a way. Think about it, Ferus. Can you imagine being able to pick and choose your own missions?"

Ferus looked at him curiously. "No. That's why we have the Council."

"But if we didn't, we could use our skills on missions that we decided were important."

"If we didn't have the Council, we wouldn't be Jedi." Ferus gave him the severe look that always got under his skin.

Anakin decided to change the subject. "Do you know anything about the planet Tierell?"

"There was a coup there. It was a repressive government. The leader was assassinated two weeks ago. The rebels are now in charge. Why?"

"The squad said they were involved," Anakin said.

"In an assassination? Do you call that a good cause?"

"I didn't say that they assassinated the leader," Anakin argued. "I just said they were involved."

"Anakin, they are mercenaries," Ferus said, exasperated. "What exactly do you think they do?"

"Not cold-blooded murder," Anakin said decidedly.

"You've made a lot of conclusions considering you just met them," Ferus said.

"It's an instinct," Anakin said. "That doesn't mean they can't be hiding something. I'm not totally in their confidence yet. I need to gain their trust."

Ferus nodded slowly. "I agree. But be careful."

Anakin said good-bye and was halfway down the hall before he wondered what exactly Ferus wanted him to be careful of.

The secret squad had a secret signal, of course. Many of the students had holographic displays outside their doors. When a hologram of a detailed topographical map of Marit's homeworld of Hali was outside her door, a meeting was scheduled. If the moons of Hali were shown, the meeting was in the free evening hours. If the three suns were shown, the meeting would take place before the morning meal.

They met almost every day. Anakin was surprised at the number of proposals for help they received, from groups and individuals all over the galaxy. The squad had only been in operation for six months, and the word of mouth had spread. Rolai received the requests on a datapad Ze had tweaked so that the routing system was too complicated to trace. Credits were deposited in a secret account in an Andoran bank known for discretion. Anakin admired the group's professionalism. They discussed the proposals seriously, and he was impressed at Marit's knowledge of galactic politics and history. It was obvious that they needed a mission soon, for their treasury was low and they needed supplies.

Anakin was heading to his last class when he saw the signal for an evening meeting. As soon as the free period began, he headed for a storeroom located near the students' rooms. The storeroom wasn't used at such hours and they did not have to pass through security checkpoints to get to it from their rooms. It was a private place to meet.

He slipped inside the room to find the others waiting. He got the sense that they had been talking before he entered. "Do we have a proposal?" he asked, sitting down on the floor next to Hurana.

"No," Rolai said. "It's just a general meeting. Anybody have anything?"

"Just stuff we can't afford," Ze said. "I haven't wanted to bring this up, but we've got to upgrade our comlinks. We've got to get some holographic capabilities pretty soon. And if we don't up-tech the drivers, we'll be blasting static when we go past the Core. I have an idea how I can do a basic upgrade without dipping into the treasury, but it's going to be complicated." Ze launched into a highly technical discussion that obviously left the rest of the squad behind.

"So if I patch into the C-board here and steal some juice from the circuit, I can maybe extend the range from meta to mega if the systems don't chatter and I don't pulverize the school mainframe," Ze concluded cheerfully.

"Affirmatively good work, Ze-tech." Tulah nodded his head in approval, but it was obvious he hadn't a clue as to what Ze was talking about. By the looks on the faces of the rest, they felt the same.

"Don't forget to bypass the transit sensor when you patch," Anakin said. "Otherwise you'll end up with a cinder instead of a comlink."

"An excellent point," Ze said, impressed.

"I was going to say that transit thing," Tulah said. "I mean, I would have if I'd known what Ze was talking about."

Marit gave Anakin a sidelong look. "You know comm systems?"

"Some," Anakin said. As a slave at Watto's shop, he had learned how to fix anything. He had kept up the hobby as a Jedi student. "I know droid circuits better."

"That's good, because we might be in the market for an astromech," Tulah said. "Love those little guys. Hurana has been shopping for a couple of used A-6 interceptors, and a couple of astromechs are key. By the way, we really need to get some starfighters soon. This hitching rides on freighters has got to stop."

"I agree," Rolai said. "They're slow."

"Right. But what I really meant was, the food is terrible," Tulah said. "Bleh."

"What's the weapon capability of the interceptors?" Rolai asked Hurana.

"Turbolaser cannons, very sweet," Hurana said. "Both ships are in good shape. The only problem is that one of them has a tendency to cut out during dives."

"That could be a minor inconvenience," Tulah said. "Remind me to fly in the other one."

Everyone laughed, but Anakin noted how their intent looks never changed. He was impressed with their focus.

"I've gone on a couple of test flights and it's a pretty consistent problem," Hurana admitted. "Last time I came within twenty meters of complete annihilation on the planet surface before I was able to pull out."

"That sounds dangerous," Anakin said. The flow of conversation was fast and decisive. It told him better than words what a tightly knit team this was.

She flashed him a grin. "That's what made it fun."

"What about a hyperdrive?" Marit asked.

Hurana shook her head. "We might be able to add it. But that means major investment capital."

"Don't worry about that," Rolai said.

"Why not?" Marit said. "The treasury is completely zilched."

"I'm working on it," Rolai said. "Just draw up your wish lists, and I'll let you know what we can handle."

"Sounds like my speed," Tulah said. "Numbers are not my thing."

"I've got a wish list, too," Rolai said. "Speaking of upgrades, our weapons are sad. A couple of blasters aren't going to get us very far. We need some secondary weaponry. Some thermal detonators, a flechette launcher, maybe some missile tubes —"

"Hang on," Marit said. "We're not an army."

"Sure we are," Rolai said. "If we act like it, we'd better have the stuff to back it up. Things would have gone a lot better on Tierell if we'd had the firepower —"

"Or a lot worse," Marit shot back.

"Not this again," Rolai said, rolling his eyes. "Six blasters for six members is the bare minimum. If we'd had a flechette launcher —"

"You're right, Rolai," Marit said. "We've gone over this too many times. Let's just be glad the mission was a success. Now we'd better get back to our rooms."

Anakin hung back as the others slipped out the door. He closed it behind them and turned to face Marit.

"We'd better get going," she said. "Lights out will be soon —"

"What was that about?" Anakin asked.

"What?" Marit said evasively.

"He said six blasters," Anakin said.

"What?"

"He said you had six blasters for six members. But there are only five."

"Six, counting you."

"But I wasn't on the mission to Tierell."

Marit shrugged. "Rolai meant now, not then. Six blasters for six members."

Anakin let it pass. "Tell me about Tierell."

Marit turned away. "I don't want to tell you about Tierell."

"Something's bothering you about it," Anakin said. "Maybe if you tell me, I can help."

"I don't need help," Marit snapped.

"Okay," Anakin said. "Then let's say I deserve to know. I'm putting my life on the line, too, you know."

Marit's brown eyes studied him. He knew the moment she decided to trust him. It only took a few seconds. He was beginning to see that Marit didn't like to waste time. "We had trouble. We'd been hired to slip into the Leader's Advisors' Chambers and dismantle security. The room was supposed to be empty, but the advisors were having a meeting. We had a battle with some security droids. The blaster fire was incredible.

We could barely handle it. And . . . in the confusion, the leader of Tierell was killed."

"Who did it?" Anakin asked.

Marit hesitated. Then she took a deep breath. "I did."

Slowly, she sank back down to a crouching position on the floor. Her hands dangled between her knees. "I've gone over it and over it, and I still don't know why or how it happened. The success of the mission depended on it. The freedom of the beings of Tierell depended on it. Maybe my friends' lives depended on it. Maybe mine. In other words . . ." Marit shrugged. "Everything depended on it. But I can't stop thinking . . ."

"That it could have gone another way." Anakin knew that feeling. He, too, had taken a life. More than one. He didn't like to think about it. Those experiences were locked in a place in his mind where he did not go.

He crouched down in front of her. "If everything depended on it, you did the right thing. If you can't make yourself believe that, you'll drive yourself crazy."

She looked into his face searchingly. "You seem to know how I feel."

"I do," Anakin said. He stood and held out his hand. She took it and he helped bring her to her feet.

"You see?" he said. "Everybody needs help sometime."

*   *   *

"I think she lied about the blasters, but I don't know why," Anakin told Obi-Wan in their next communication.

"Do you think Gillam was once part of the squad?"

"That doesn't make sense. He's not a scholarship student. But something is up, I can feel it. Something with Rolai isn't right. Maybe he knows something. He's in charge of security, and also the treasury. None of the others seem to care about how he handles it. Maybe . . . I don't know, maybe he decided to raise money by kidnapping Gillam and holding him for ransom, but he didn't tell the others."

"Maybe," Obi-Wan said doubtfully. He sounded distracted, as though he weren't really listening to Anakin. "But Tarturi hasn't received a ransom demand."

"Yet. I'm not sure what to think," Anakin confessed. "I can't imagine the group kidnapping Gillam. They're all pretty dedicated. Marit has an incredible grasp of galactic politics. She knows what's being debated in the Senate right down to the subcommittee hearings. And she always comes in on the right side."

"And how do you know it's the right side?" Obi-Wan asked, his voice dry. "Because you agree with it?"

"Because they are against violence and oppression," Anakin said. "They're like the Jedi."

"Yet they are operating against school rules," Obi-Wan pointed out. "If you are willing to violate trust, you cannot claim virtue."

"The school doesn't deserve their trust. It let them down."

"Nonetheless, they are attending the school and agreed to abide by its rules," Obi-Wan said. "I can understand the attraction they have for you, Anakin, but I fear you are getting too involved. You must be a Jedi at all times. You must constantly strive for inner balance. This includes being swayed by the ideas of others. They often mask a different purpose."

"What purpose could they mask?"

"That is your job to find out. Do not forget that you are trying to find a missing boy. Anakin, the fact that you are a Jedi is what will keep you steady always. That is something to hold on to. If you know your first loyalty, the rest falls into place. Do you understand?"

"I do, Master. Have you made progress in the Senate?"

Obi-Wan sighed. "Yes and no. Nothing to report yet. I'm sure there is a connection between Rana Halion and Sano Sauro, but I can't find it."

"Rana Halion?"

"Ruler of Ieria. The leader of the countermovement

in that system. I think she might have something to do with Gillam's disappearance. Keep me informed if you learn anything more, Padawan."

"Yes, Master." Anakin frowned as Obi-Wan cut the communication. His Master had not been very forthcoming with information. And he did not seem interested in the secret squad. Anakin had the feeling that Obi-Wan didn't think they were involved in Gillam's disappearance.

But Anakin felt differently. And here, he could follow his own rules.

All his life, he had known only two ways to live: as a slave, or as a Jedi. As a young boy on Tatooine he had looked to the Jedi as the most free beings in the galaxy. Even before he knew much about them, he had dreamed of being a Jedi.

But was being a Jedi being free? Or had he traded one form of slavery for another?

The thought was so shocking that Anakin couldn't face it once he dredged it up. He tucked it away in the place in his mind that he did not visit. It was a place where fear ruled. He never went there, not even in the middle of the night when he woke, his head full of dreams, and did not know where he was or why his mother was not near.

Anakin put his comlink back into his tunic. For the first time since entering the school, returning to comm silence did not make him feel cut off. He was glad not to answer to anyone, even for twenty-four hours. He headed out to find Marit and the squad, where there were no Masters to chide him.

CHAPTER TEN

Frustration boiled inside Obi-Wan. He could not trace a connection between Sano Sauro and Rana Halion. He was working on it; Tyro was working on it. The best researchers at the Temple were working on it, including Jocasta Nu, the Jedi Archivist. Though she usually demanded that Jedi Knights do their own research, she agreed to help Obi-Wan since the matter was so pressing. A young boy's life could be at stake. The image of Gillam still tore at Obi-Wan's heart — the way he'd clutched the blanket around his shoulders, the courage he tried to convey.

None of these experts had come up with anything. And Obi-Wan was plagued by the feeling that he was missing something. Something obvious.

He retreated to his private quarters to think. He felt

more in need of a Master than Anakin. He wished someone could give him the direction he was looking for.

In his reports from the Leadership School, Anakin had sounded self-sufficient, completely in charge of the situation. Obi-Wan didn't know if the secret squad was involved in Gillam's disappearance, but he was proud of his Padawan for infiltrating it so quickly. He just wished he hadn't heard something in Anakin's voice that reminded him of his own past. When he had been a Padawan, he had briefly left the Jedi after meeting a rebel group on Melida/Daan called The Young. To him, The Young had passion and commitment and an important cause. When Qui-Gon had forbidden him to stay and help them, he had turned his back on the Jedi. It had made complete sense to him then. He had felt so right — and he had been so wrong.

Inner balance. It took experience to know when the wrong instinct had made it careen off-kilter.

But Anakin was not the same. Being a Jedi meant everything to Anakin.

Obi-Wan returned to his more pressing problem. He stared down at the security report once again. What was he missing? He had a feeling that Qui-Gon would know. His Master was always able to combine emotion with logic to reach the correct conclusion. *Find the emo-*

tion behind the logic — or the illogic, Qui-Gon would say. If you can't see the solution, try to see the emotion. But if something seemed logical to Obi-Wan, it was difficult to see the illogical heart of it.

He heard Qui-Gon's voice clearly in his head. If something is not possible, then it did not happen.

Obi-Wan stood up so suddenly that the report slid off his lap. Security wasn't breached. Gillam never left the academy campus!

He was still there. But was he alive . . . or dead? And who took him?

Ferus had reported that Reymet had hinted that he knew how to visit places he wasn't supposed to go within the school campus. What if Reymet wasn't just trying to impress Ferus? What if Reymet had seen something that night?

Obi-Wan shook his head. It didn't seem logical that Reymet would keep silent when the life of a fellow student was at stake. Reymet might be a sneak, but he had no reason to suppose he would support a kidnapper.

Obi-Wan had never attended a regular school, but the Temple was like one in many ways. He thought back to his own training. Why would Reymet keep silent?

The answer roared into his brain.

Because adults didn't take Gillam. Students did. A boy Reymet's age wouldn't turn in fellow students. What had Anakin told him students called someone who snitched?

If Reymet told, he'd be a womp fink.

His comlink signaled. Hoping it was Anakin, he snatched it and activated it.

He felt the thud of disappointment when he heard Jocastu Nu's voice. Unless Anakin contacted him on the emergency channel, he would have to wait until their next scheduled communication the following day.

"I have traced the payment for you, even though you were perfectly capable of doing so yourself, if you had paid attention to my instructions," Jocasta Nu's crisp voice said. "There was a credit payment from Rana Halion to an account on Andara. The account is anonymous, but through a series of traces I've discovered that it is used by that secret renegade squad the Council is so concerned about. A boy named Rolai Frac set it up. An impressive use of cloaking maneuvers hid his identity. I've rarely seen better."

"Thank you, Madame Nu," Obi-Wan said fervently.

"Next time, you will do your own research, Master Kenobi. I do not have time to indulge your many requests, and I —"

"Yes, Madame Nu," Obi-Wan said. "May the Force be with you. You may have just given me the key to find the boy."

"That's good, then. May the Force be with you," she answered, the disapproval fading from her voice.

It was the confirmation he needed. Anakin's hunch that the secret squad was involved was right after all. Gillam had been kidnapped by his fellow students on the secret squad. But they hadn't done it on their own — Rana Halion had arranged it. Whether Sano Sauro was involved, he might never know.

Obi-Wan hurried out of his quarters toward the vehicle requisition area. He felt as though he should kick himself down the hall. He had chastised Anakin about inner balance while he was losing his own! His need to investigate Sano Sauro had led him to make assumptions and go off on a dangerous tack. He had wanted Sauro to be responsible, so he had tried to build a case around it.

He had been so wrong. He had lost sight of his goal: to find the missing boy. The answer wasn't at the Senate. It was on Andara.

CHAPTER ELEVEN

Anakin left his room well before the call for the morning meal. There was no hologram on Marit's door. He hesitated, fighting his urge to knock. It was unusual for the squad not to meet again. There had been several things to resolve. And he'd had the feeling that Marit was avoiding him.

He left without knocking, however, and continued down the hall. Maybe Ferus had some new information. Anakin was beginning to get impatient. Days were passing, and they were no closer to finding Gillam.

He was almost at Ferus's door when he saw the door to the athletic storeroom slide open. Rolai stepped out.

Anakin quickly retreated back around the corner. He peered around the wall and saw Tulah, Hurana, and Ze

89

hurrying out behind Rolai. They all disappeared around the corner.

Anakin strode forward and pushed open the door. Marit was just tucking her datapad under her arm. She looked at him, startled.

"What's going on?" he demanded. "I thought I was in the squad. Why am I being left out?"

"We don't know if we can completely trust you yet, Anakin," Marit said reluctantly.

"You've accepted a new mission, haven't you?" Anakin guessed.

Marit nodded, biting her lip.

Exasperated, Anakin turned on his heel. "Fine. I'm out."

"Anakin, wait!" Marit put her hand on his arm.

"It's Rolai, isn't it? He doesn't want me in the squad."

"No, Rolai is the one who wants you on the mission," Marit said. "It's just that I think it's dangerous, and it might not be the right way to start."

"Just tell me, and let me decide," Anakin said.

"It's a mission very close by," she said. "Right here in the Andaran system. You might not know this, but there's a countermovement here."

"I've heard something about it," Anakin said.

She gave him a keen look. "How do you stand on the issue?"

Anakin shrugged. "I don't know enough about it."

"Andara is the largest and richest planet in the system," Marit said. "As a result, it has grabbed the best trade routes and built up its manufacturing and exporting to the detriment of the other planets in the system. They aren't fairly represented by their Senator. They can't get what they need from the Senate because they don't have a voice."

"That doesn't seem fair," Anakin said.

"It's not. A representative of the countermovement came to us and asked for our help."

"Who?"

"You don't need to know that yet."

Anakin started for the door again.

"All right!" Marit's voice was amused, and she was smiling when he turned. "You're very tough."

He grinned. "Yeah. But isn't that why you recruited me?"

"It's Rana Halion, the leader of Ieria. She approached us through Rolai. The countermovement is willing to negotiate with Berm Tarturi, but the Senator hasn't taken them seriously enough. They want to show him how powerful they are."

Rana Halion! This could be the connection Obi-Wan was looking for.

"How?" Anakin asked.

"They want to conduct a passive strike on the Andaran security transport landing platform," Marit said.

"Passive strike?"

"We're just going to penetrate their airspace and then get out. Buzz the starfighters. Show Tarturi that we *could* have destroyed his fleet if we'd wanted to. That way he'd be forced to join negotiations. We need to get in and get out quickly. There could be some antispacecraft fire." She hesitated.

Anakin waited.

"We were going to vote on whether to include you tonight," Marit said.

Anakin said nothing. He had learned from Obi-Wan that not asking a question sometimes got you more information.

"We need a pilot," Marit said. "Hurana is good, but she's not as good as she thinks she is. She takes too many chances. We need a lead pilot. But this won't be on a simulator. Ieria is loaning us the air transport. I don't expect you've ever flown a starfighter, have you?"

"As a matter of fact, I have," Anakin said.

"Are you as good in a starfighter as you are in a swoop?"

"Better."

"I can talk to them . . . convince the others . . . if you're sure you want to go."

"I'm sure," Anakin said. He wanted to go on the mission. If the planets in the Andaran system were being exploited, they should have a voice in their destiny. Marit's ideas made sense to him. He had been a witness to the greed of Senators. It sounded as though Ieria needed help.

"Well, I'm not authorized to tell you that you can go," Marit said. She grinned. "But you're on board. We're scheduled to leave tomorrow."

Elation roared through Anakin. Then he realized something startling. He hadn't been glad because of the Jedi mission. He'd been glad because he wanted to go. Not for the Jedi. For himself.

CHAPTER TWELVE

Anakin was filled with excitement about the coming mission. He had a strong feeling that not only would he help the Andaran system, he would also discover the key to Gillam's disappearance. Rana Halion must be behind it. Her cause might be just, but her methods could be ruthless. Anakin felt sure that Gillam was on Ieria.

He saw Ferus in the hall between classes and signaled that he needed to talk to him. They met in Ferus's room and closed the door. They had a few minutes before the midday meal before they needed to pass the checkpoint to the dining hall.

Anakin quickly filled in Ferus on what had happened.

Ferus frowned. "You told Marit that you would go?"

"I think I should," Anakin said. "I still have a feeling about Gillam."

"That's fine," Ferus said. "But penetrating a planet's airspace? You can't do that."

"No one will be hurt."

"How can you be sure of that? Are you saying that no one will fire their laser cannons? Are you saying that if they fire on you or the others, you won't fire back? Think about it, Anakin! And what about the reaction in the Senate? This will be seen as an unprovoked attack on Andara."

"Not unprovoked," Anakin argued. "Senator Tarturi refuses to negotiate a compromise. This will force him to."

Ferus shook his head. "Jedi can't take part in such things. Have you told Obi-Wan this?"

"No," Anakin admitted. "Our next scheduled communication isn't until tonight."

"We can use the emergency signaling system," Ferus said.

"But that could blow our cover! We're on comm silence. The school could trace the frequency."

"We have to risk it," Ferus said. "I can't believe that you even considered going without consulting him. Even *you* should know that —"

"Even *me*?" Anakin took a step toward Ferus, angry now. "What does that mean, Ferus?"

Ferus went very still. "A personal argument is not productive," he said stiffly. "Will you meet me later and contact Obi-Wan?"

Anakin counted several beats of his tripping heart. He accepted his anger and tried to let it go. He pictured it leaving him like a black storm cloud blown by a high wind, but traces of it clung to him and he could not shake it off.

"Yes," he said reluctantly.

He left and hurried toward the dining hall. He sat with Marit and Hurana. Hurana was quiet, but Marit was in high spirits. They did not talk about the mission ahead, but the secret lay between them, giving a charge to their conversation. He could see that Marit had accepted him fully into the squad. She trusted him now.

But you're going to betray that trust.

Was he? He hoped not. But the time was coming when he would have to leave the school and the squad.

Anakin went to his next class so that he would not be missed and compromise the squad. Then he faked an illness and started toward the med clinic. Their emergency plan was for Ferus to also fake a reason to leave class. They were to meet in his room.

Ferus wasn't there. Anakin waited, watching the clock, knowing that he was pushing his luck. When Ferus didn't appear, Anakin hurried to his next class. He would see Ferus there, and he hoped to get a chance to ask him why he had insisted on a meeting he didn't show up for. Maybe he was busy polishing his utility belt.

Anakin took his usual seat. He glanced over, but Ferus's seat was empty. The professor began, but Anakin couldn't listen. Ferus's seat remained empty. Suddenly, Anakin was seriously worried.

After class, Anakin walked quickly through the halls. He searched the library, Ferus's room, and all the class-rooms. He searched the athletic fields and the re-search centers and the computer labs. He casually asked Reymet if he'd seen him, but Reymet hadn't, either.

Ferus had disappeared.

Anakin could not believe it. Security had not been violated. No one had seen Ferus, not even Reymet. It was just like Gillam's disappearance. If Ferus hadn't shown up for class, it would have been reported. Soon the school would be involved. Security would tighten even further.

He would have to contact Obi-Wan. The disappearance of a Jedi was a matter for the whole Council, not merely his Master.

Still, Anakin hesitated. It was hard to be certain that Ferus had truly disappeared. What if he was chasing a lead and hadn't told Anakin? Anakin knew it would be out of character for Ferus not to fill him in, but Ferus might be teaching him a lesson after Anakin hadn't asked his opinion about going off with the squad.

Yet if Anakin violated comm silence, he risked the whole school being put into lockdown. How would the secret squad be able to get out then?

Marit found him in the library during his free mod period, still debating the issue in his mind.

"We've moved up the mission," she whispered. "We're leaving now. We all signed out for leave. If you're coming, you'd better do it, too. I'll come with you. We made up a research trip to the library in Utare and got Professor Totem to sign a pass for us."

Anakin hesitated.

"Aren't you coming?" Marit asked. She frowned. "Did you change your mind? I know the mission sounds dangerous."

Anakin felt the conflict inside him as though he was being physically torn apart. He knew his duty as a Jedi. He had to inform Obi-Wan about Ferus. But if his suspicions were correct and the answers were on Ieria, that meant he could find out answers about Ferus's disappearance as well. If he broke comm silence he could jeopardize everything. His only chance to find Ferus and possibly Gillam was to maintain his cover.

"I didn't change my mind," Anakin said. "Let's go."

CHAPTER THIRTEEN

Obi-Wan landed his starship on the main public landing platform in Utare. He completed his postflight check and activated the landing ramp. As he strode down it, he saw Siri waiting at the bottom. Her hands were on her hips and her blue eyes sparked fire.

He guessed that she did not have good news.

She spoke when he was still only halfway down the ramp. "How could you withhold this from me, Obi-Wan? Did you think you could solve it by yourself and I'd never have to know? Were you afraid of how I'd react?" She put one booted foot on the ramp as though she were ready to charge at him. "Well, you were right to be afraid!"

"Nice to see you, too, Siri," Obi-Wan said, coming up

to her. He had been friends with Siri for over ten years now, and she could still nettle him like no one else. He wondered what minor infraction he was guilty of. "Now, do you mind filling me in on what you're talking about?"

"Ferus is missing!" she exclaimed. "Don't tell me you didn't know."

Obi-Wan's mild amusement faded immediately. "No, I didn't."

"Didn't Anakin contact you?"

"Our next scheduled communication isn't until tonight, and I received no emergency signal. Are you sure about this?"

"Ferus contacted me via the emergency channel. I was on a mission and couldn't answer for an hour. When I tried to reach him, he didn't answer."

"He never sent me a signal," Obi-Wan said.

"I think something happened before he could," Siri said. "His message was cut off. But he did say that Anakin was taking off on a mission with the secret squad. They're going to conduct an air strike on the Andaran security transport landing platform."

Obi-Wan stopped short. "What?"

"You didn't know?"

"Of course not." Obi-Wan was staggered by this news. He couldn't absorb it. A Jedi was missing, and

Anakin had not informed him? Anakin had agreed to take part in an air strike against a nonhostile planet? It seemed inconceivable.

"I don't understand," he said. "Was Anakin captured, or forced to leave with the squad?"

"No," Siri said. "It was his own free will. Ferus was clear about that. He sounded worried about Anakin."

Ferus was often worried about Anakin, Obi-Wan thought. He had noted that already. Ferus was concerned that Anakin would let down the Order in some way.

And so he had. Obi-Wan felt the betrayal like a hard blow to his stomach. He had trouble getting air. He struggled with his own emotions, surprised at the depth of them. He felt betrayed, he realized. Why hadn't Anakin trusted him?

He swallowed. "Did Ferus know where Anakin was headed?"

"To Ieria. That's all. And it's a big planet."

He wished Siri would look away. Her eyes had not left his face. Her gaze scorched him.

He had promised to watch over Ferus like his own Padawan. He had failed.

He had lost both Padawans. It was unthinkable. Yet here he was.

He did not know what to do. Whatever step he took

could be the wrong one. And if he took the wrong one, he could lose one of them. Or both.

Obi-Wan's thoughts whirled crazily. He could not focus.

"Let's decide how to proceed," Siri said crisply.

That was the way of the Jedi. Accept the mistake and move on. But Obi-Wan's mind was a blank.

"We need to get into the school," Siri said. "Ferus is still there. I feel it."

The confusion cleared, and Obi-Wan remembered why he had come to Andara.

"I think Gillam is there, too," he said. "But without Anakin and Ferus to help us, we can't infiltrate the campus without being detected. We can't come as Jedi. We can't take the chance that someone will be watching. We must appear as though we belong there."

"But how?" Siri asked. "Security there is incredibly tight. And we don't look like students."

"I have an idea," Obi-Wan said.

Siri gave him a searching look. "I can tell I'm not going to like it."

"You're going to hate it," Obi-Wan said.

"Your excellencies," the president of the school said graciously. "How kind of you to consider the Leadership School for your son."

Obi-Wan and Siri walked into the inner office. It had taken only minutes to contact Tyro for some fast false text docs.

"Thank you for seeing us on such short notice," Obi-Wan said.

"The king and queen of Cortella are always welcome," the president said. "Now, how old is your son?"

"Thirteen," Obi-Wan said.

"Eleven," Siri said at the same time.

They looked at each other.

"Two sons," Obi-Wan said quickly. "We have two. One for each of us," he added heartily.

"I see. And you wish to enroll both?"

"No," Siri said.

"Yes," Obi-Wan said at the same time.

"Remember, we talked about this, uh, dear?" Siri said, her eyes flashing a warning at Obi-Wan.

Obi-Wan tried not to smile. He couldn't help enjoying how much Siri was hating this.

"Of course. But you agreed with me, as you always do," he said.

Siri's gaze flashed sparks at Obi-Wan, but the president could not see. Siri inclined her head haughtily. She hadn't done much to change her appearance, merely slicked back her hair more severely, but she looked suddenly regal to Obi-Wan.

"Nevertheless, it remains to be seen whether the princes will both attend," she said in a distant tone. "We must be assured, of course, that the school is up to the highest standard."

"It must be suitable for our royal regal sons," Obi-Wan said. Siri shot him a look that said, *Let me handle this.*

"Of course," the president said nervously. "Shall we get started on our tour?"

Obi-Wan and Siri stood. "We would prefer to tour on our own," Obi-Wan said.

"We feel we will absorb the spirit of the place in that manner," Siri said. She indicated their traveler's tunics. "We dressed this way precisely so that we would not be conspicuous. We will not disturb your students."

"Uh, ah . . . this is not exactly customary . . ." the president stammered.

"Nevertheless, it is our wish," Obi-Wan said in a tone that implied that he was not used to being overruled.

"If there is a problem, we will go elsewhere," Siri said. "There is an excellent school on Alderaan —"

"No, no, no problem," the president said. He waved a hand. "You are free to explore. I will alert security that you are not to be disturbed."

Siri tilted her head again. Obi-Wan nodded. They swept out the door.

"If you ever get tired of being a Jedi, you'd make an amazing queen," Obi-Wan told Siri as soon as the door had slid shut behind them.

"And you'd make a terrible king," she said. "Royal regal sons?"

"I was trying to sound pompous," Obi-Wan said.

"Do you really think you need to try?" Siri asked. Her clear blue eyes held a mischievous glint. In the middle of any crisis, Siri was always able to joke. It never failed to take him by surprise. Now he realized with a sense of relief that her teasing was designed to tell him that she did not hold him responsible for the disappearance of Ferus. He was grateful to his old friend. He knew her so well. She would not speak of her feelings, but she would always manage to let him know what they were.

"Did you notice that the president seemed nervous?" Obi-Wan asked. "And it wasn't just because he was meeting with a king and queen. The school must know Ferus is missing."

"And they want to keep it quiet," Siri said, nodding. "That's why they haven't put the school in lockdown. If it's discovered that there are two missing students, they could lose students . . . and revenue."

"Exactly. But the school must be looking for Ferus, too. They'll search the obvious places."

"So we have to get to the un-obvious ones," Siri said. "Where should we start?"

"I think we should try to find Reymet Autem," Obi-Wan said. "Ferus said several times that Reymet hinted at knowing something about Gillam's disappearance. And he also said he knew how to get around security. Ferus never found out if he really did, but . . ."

"He's our only lead," Siri finished.

They started down the halls. Most of the students were in class. The president must have alerted security, for they were waved through all checkpoints.

But with the halls empty, they would have no luck finding Reymet. "We're not getting anywhere," Siri said, frustrated. "Maybe we need to go to registration. We can think of something in order to gain access to the class schedules —"

"I don't think that's necessary," Obi-Wan said. "You're forgetting the best thing about classes."

"What's that?"

A soft beeping signal came over the hidden speakers.

"They end," Obi-Wan said.

Just then a voice was broadcast, speaking in a quiet but insistent tone. "End of mod six class. Five minutes to mod seven. Five minutes."

Suddenly the doors hissed open and students

spilled out into the hall. Obi-Wan and Siri were pushed against the walls as students ran, jostled, tossed datapads at one another playfully, or wolfed down a quick snack as they walked. Yet both Jedi could feel the effort and bravado in the calls and laughter. These students were afraid.

Obi-Wan hailed a student who appeared to be about Anakin and Ferus's age. "Excuse me. Do you know Reymet Autem?"

The tall Phlog nodded. "He's in my Current Galactic Political Trends class."

"Can you find him for us?" Siri asked.

"Not a problem. He's right there." The Phlog pointed to a boy across the hall who was tossing a small datapad from one hand to the other as he walked.

"Thanks." It was a lucky break. Obi-Wan and Siri headed toward Reymet.

"Are you a friend of Ferus Olin?" Siri asked him.

Reymet nodded proudly. "We're best friends." He eyed them carefully. "Hey, are you his parents? You look like you could be."

"Yes, we're his parents," Siri said. "Have you seen him this afternoon?"

"No, and that's weird, because he's in three of my classes," Reymet said. "Is he sick?"

"No, Reymet," Obi-Wan said. "That's why we came

to you. We think Ferus is missing. We think it has something to do with what happened to Gillam Tarturi."

"Will you help us?" Siri asked. "Ferus told us that you know secret things about the school."

"I know some things," Reymet said cautiously.

"We promise we won't tell the school officials anything you show us," Siri said.

Reymet still hesitated. "Unless you don't tell us anything, and then we'd be forced to go to the school officials," Obi-Wan pointed out.

"Whoa," Reymet said. "In that case, I'd be happy to tell you everything I know."

Obi-Wan noted that he sounded relieved. Maybe Reymet had a secret that had been a burden to keep, and that was why he kept hinting to Ferus that he knew something. "Follow me."

The halls were emptying of students as Reymet quickly led them down to the ground level of the school.

"Class beginning. Mod seven." The soft voice floated out from the speakers. "Mod seven. Class beginning."

The hallway was empty. "Hurry," Reymet hissed. "I only have a few minutes before I have to check in to my next class."

He ducked into a storage closet, and Obi-Wan and Siri quickly followed. They crowded in next to him.

"Couldn't you find a bigger place for us to hide?" Obi-Wan asked as he bumped into a durasteel toolbox.

"If you could just squeeze together, I can . . ." Reymet began to wiggle past them, then ducked down below them. ". . . okay, just a second . . . move your foot . . . no, the other way . . . thanks . . ."

Reymet unscrewed a panel from the wall. A large utility shaft opened up.

"In there," he said.

"What's in there?" Obi-Wan asked, peering in.

"When they renovated, they just built around all the old electrical and water systems," Reymet explained. "It was cheaper than ripping them out. There's a whole network of utility pipes still in place. They lead to the old system rooms."

"Did you show Ferus this?" Siri asked.

Reymet nodded. "We were going to explore it together, during free time. I didn't know he was missing. I would have looked for him —"

"Do you think he's with Gillam?" Obi-Wan asked. He kept his gaze on Reymet.

Whatever reserve the young boy had crumbled. "I don't know," he said. "I think Gillam is still here, though. I saw him the night he disappeared. He knew about the old utility pipes, too."

"Do you think Gillam is hiding?" Siri asked.

Reymet nodded. "I don't blame him. With a father like that, I'd hide, too. That's why I wouldn't tell on him." He looked uneasily at them. "But now I'm not so sure. I can see Gillam hiding, but I can't see Ferus doing that. He isn't mean like Gillam."

"Gillam is mean?" Obi-Wan asked.

"Maybe I shouldn't have said that," Reymet said. "He's not mean, I guess. He's just . . . not nice." He shifted from one foot to the other uneasily. It was clear he was worried he'd said too much. "They're doing extra security checks — and I'm late for class. One more demerit and I'm suspended. Not that having to leave this place would break my heart. But it just might break my old man."

"Go," Obi-Wan told him. "We'll handle it from here."

Reymet suddenly looked lost. "I really hope you find him. I like him a lot." Reymet hurried out the door.

Obi-Wan peered into the pipe. He could see where the dust had been disturbed, but it was impossible to tell by whom or by how many.

"After you," Siri said.

Obi-Wan climbed into the pipe. He had to stoop and move slowly because of his size. Siri had an easier time.

"Hurry," she urged him.

"Would you like to go first?"

"If I could get around you, I would."

Obi-Wan saw light at the end of the pipe and quickened his pace. He slid out of the pipe onto a springy floor. He realized that it was covered in moss. The large space had a damp, moldy smell. Mildew marked the walls in cloudy patterns. The smell was close and dank.

"This must have been some sort of holding tank," Siri said. She took out a glow rod and held it up. "Makes sense if that was a water pipe."

Obi-Wan felt the floor suck at his boots. "There's a couple of passageways. Any ideas?" He turned to Siri, but he already felt the Force move in the space. She was looking keenly about her, sending out the Force, trying to reach her Padawan. Obi-Wan joined her, calling on the Force to help them locate Ferus.

They turned at the same moment and headed for the passageway to their left. They could feel it now. The Force had entered the dank, dark space, and they knew Ferus was near.

Siri held her glow rod aloft. "I think we're in the old water treatment system. See the inflow pipes?"

"These are holding pens for the water," Obi-Wan said, peering into the rooms as they passed. Some of the chambers still had their durasteel panel doors. Others had doors that were half rusted away, or had been removed.

The Force grew stronger. Ahead they saw a chamber with an intact door. It was bolted to the wall with a new lock.

Siri withdrew her lightsaber. Within seconds, the metal peeled back, giving them an entry to the chamber.

Ferus sat in the middle of the room. He quickly stood, facing them. "I am sorry for needing rescue, Master," he said to Siri. "I am sorry, Master Kenobi."

"We all need rescue sometime," Obi-Wan said.

"Some more than others," Siri said, grinning at Obi-Wan.

Ferus was so different from Anakin, Obi-Wan thought. Anakin would have smiled at him as soon as he entered. *It's about time,* he would have said. Or maybe, *I hope you brought my lunch.* He felt an intense need to find his own Padawan. Added to the feeling was the fury that he was gone at all.

"What happened?" Siri asked Ferus. "Are you all right? Where is your lightsaber?"

"It's hidden in my room." Ferus made a face. "One of several of my mistakes. I came down here looking for Gillam without stopping there first. I thought if I found him I could prevent Anakin taking off with the secret squad. Instead, Gillam found me."

"Gillam?" Obi-Wan asked, surprised.

Ferus nodded. "He was never kidnapped. He staged it himself."

Obi-Wan felt a surge of impatience. He should have examined this possibility. He hadn't been able to imagine a son doing such a thing to his father. No matter how much he'd seen in his life, no matter what evil he'd faced, he was still capable of surprise at a son's resentment of a powerful father. It always surprised him, how personal a betrayal could be.

"I don't understand how he could have imprisoned you," Siri said with a frown.

"I was exploring, and I found a hiding place," Ferus said. "It's just down this corridor. His datapad was hidden in a drain behind a lock, in a plastoid sleeve. I was just trying to access it when I heard someone coming. It was Gillam and a few members of the secret squad. I was able to conceal the datapad but they got my comlink."

"What did they do?" Obi-Wan asked. He felt dread invade him. So the secret squad was involved.

"They thought I was just a nosy student," Ferus said. "I decided not to resist because I didn't want to blow my cover, or especially Anakin's. They didn't know what to do with me. They were afraid I'd report them. They searched me, but I used the Force to redirect them, so I was able to hang onto Gillam's datapad. Then they put me in here. Gillam brought me food, but I haven't seen him in hours."

Ferus held up the datapad. "They left me alone, so I was able to read this. First of all, look — it has a Senate seal."

Obi-Wan took it. He recognized the symbol of Andara on the back. "This belongs to Berm Tarturi." He thought a moment. "Maybe Tarturi was right. Someone *did* break into his office and go through his things. But it was his own son."

Ferus nodded. "That's not all. There are ransom notes on this pad. Two of them have been sent. I think Gillam plans to pin his own kidnapping on his father."

"Why would he do such a thing?" Siri asked. "Does he hate him so much?"

"He must," Ferus said. "But that's not the only thing. Are you in contact with Anakin?"

Obi-Wan shook his head. "He hasn't reported in. He must be traveling or even on Ieria by now, but his comlink has been turned off."

Ferus looked grave. "The last letter in the file takes responsibility for Gillam's death. It hasn't been sent yet, but it's timed to go out in five hours."

"He's going to frame his father for his own murder?" Obi-Wan said.

"But how?" Siri asked. "He'll need a body. There will be some kind of investigation."

"That's what I've been thinking about," Ferus said quietly. He ran his hands through his hair in a rare gesture of agitation. "What if Gillam planned to produce a body? Someone similar in age and build, someone who looks a little like him. They could plant text docs on the body, or near it."

"They'd have to count on a great deal of chaos and confusion," Siri said. "There are many tests that can be done to determine identity."

"The secret squad is going to help start a war between Andara and the rest of the planets in the system," Obi-Wan said. "They may not realize it, but they will. That will certainly create chaos." He suddenly realized what Ferus, brooding in this damp cell, had already put together. "They just need a body." He thought back to the information he had on Gillam, to the boy's height and weight and coloring. "And they've chosen —"

"Anakin," Ferus said.

CHAPTER FOURTEEN

"If this doesn't work, I don't know you," Rana Halion said. Her spiky white hair seemed to bristle like fur as she surveyed the secret squad.

Marit nodded. "Understood."

"But it had better work," Rana Halion added.

"It will," Rolai said.

Rana Halion's transparent blue eyes swept the group. She sighed. "If you didn't come so highly recommended, I wouldn't believe it," she murmured. "You look like a bunch of kids."

Anakin had to agree. Rolai was skinny and pale beneath his Bothan mane. Ze was plump. Tulah always looked as though he had just woken from a nap, and Hurana appeared slight and shy.

But he had seen that Rolai was tough, almost ruthless, Ze could dissect and solve any technical problem in five minutes or less, Tulah had a brilliant mind for strategy, and Hurana had convictions and no fear. Marit was smart and resourceful. He would put his own trust in this squad.

Rana pushed a contact button on her gold cuff and watched as a digital coded message flashed at her.

"I don't have much time. Who is your lead pilot?"

Anakin stepped forward. "I am."

Rana looked at him intently. Anakin thought it could have been the most intimidating glance he'd ever experienced — if he hadn't grown up at the Temple. Once you've faced Jedi like Mace Windu, no one else could intimidate you. He did not drop his own gaze and met hers without flinching.

She gave a short nod. "You seem competent. Can you pilot a starfighter?"

"I can fly anything."

"I almost believe it," she murmured, giving him another glance. "Do you know how to fire laser cannons at a target?"

Anakin glanced at Marit. "I thought there was to be no active firing."

Rana looked exasperated. "Who's in charge here?"

"We all are," Rolai broke in crisply. "And we all know how to fire laser cannons. We've been over this."

"Have you thoroughly briefed the squad?" Rana asked, raising an eyebrow skeptically.

"Not with the final details," Rolai said smoothly. "We were waiting for the exact time of departure and target details."

Rana glanced at her cuff again. "Do it then. You can inspect the starfighters. You leave in thirty minutes."

Marit exploded as soon as Rana was out of the room. "What was that all about? What do you mean, you haven't briefed the squad? What do you know that we don't know? We're supposed to vote on everything!"

"Calm down," Rolai said with a glance at the door to make sure Rana was out of earshot.

"Don't tell me to calm down," Marit answered hotly. "Tell me the truth!"

"The mission just changed a bit," Rolai said. "We're supposed to fire on the fleet."

"Fire on the fleet?" Anakin asked. "But that's a declaration of war!"

"That's not our problem," Rolai said. "We're hired to do the job. That's all."

"Wait," Marit said. "Why didn't you tell us this?" She looked at Ze, Hurana, and Tulah. Their gazes slid away. "You all knew, and I didn't?"

"I didn't know, either," Anakin pointed out.

But no one was paying attention to Anakin. "We all voted to wait to tell you until we got here," Hurana said. She didn't meet Marit's hot gaze.

"We thought you might object," Rolai said. "After the last mission, you had some misgivings about organic damage."

"Organic damage?" Marit said in disbelief. "Is that what you're calling it now? They were living beings!"

"Marit, what do you think we're doing?" Rolai asked. "This isn't school. It isn't a game. We all agreed we would start this as a business and run it as a business. We all agreed that we would make our own destinies."

"That's the point," Marit said angrily. "We *all* agreed. We didn't leave someone out."

"I get your point, Marit," Rolai said. "Now let's move on. Here we are. Are you going to join us, or not?"

Anakin watched Marit's face. He could see that she was torn. No one cared what he thought, but he would throw his support behind Marit if she voted to back out.

"I'm in," she said in a low tone.

The group looked relieved. Even Rolai did, although he tried to hide it.

"Hold on," Anakin said. "What about me? I'm part of the squad. Don't I get a vote, too?"

Rolai gave him a glance that was so neutral Anakin felt a chill. It was as though Anakin wasn't even there.

"We don't have time for this," Rolai said. "Let's inspect the starfighters."

Rana Halion suddenly appeared again. "We have a slight change in the timing of the attack. We need to go over the coordinates and warning systems now. You'll have to come to the briefing room."

Rolai gestured to the group. "Let's go."

"While you're doing that, I'll check out the starfighters," Anakin said. "I need to look at the controls and see if I can handle them."

Rolai gave him a glance. "I thought you said you could fly anything," he hissed so that Rana could not hear.

Anakin shrugged. "I sure *hope* I can," he murmured. "I don't tell you everything. But then again, you don't tell me everything, either. Do you?"

Rolai shot him a murderous look. "We're coming," he called to Halion. "You," he whispered angrily to Anakin, "check out those starfighters. You're going to have to give the rest of us some quick lessons."

Anakin waited until the group had left with Rana. Then he hurried to the hangar. There wasn't much time. He didn't have a choice now. He couldn't let the mission go through. He had to disable those starfighters. He knew that now. He was nowhere near discovering what happened to Ferus or Gillam, and he was about to start a war. He was probably breaking every Jedi rule in the archives.

The Ierian starfighters were modifications of the Delta-6 *Aethersprite* that he was used to. Anakin knew every bolt on the engine. He thought for a minute. He needed to disable something that would show up as a warning light midflight but wouldn't put the ship in danger. He wanted to give the pilots plenty of time to turn around and land. It would have to be something that would immediately lead them to abort the mission.

The laser cannon capacitors. Anakin swung open the maintenance panel. Small tools were snapped onto the panel within easy reach. He selected a small servo-driver and within minutes had disabled the capacitators.

He started toward the next ship, wondering if he should alter the engine cooling system just enough to cause the engines to overheat slightly. That might add a little urgency to the decision to abort the mission . . .

"What are you doing?"

Marit's voice echoed across the hangar. Anakin paused and peered around the control panel.

"Just a little tweaking."

She walked forward and peered into the system controls. "Do you think I'm stupid, Anakin? You've neutralized the laser cannon capacitators. I've studied the blueprints of this engine. I came back to see if you needed help. I guess you don't, do you?" She turned and looked at him. Their faces were very close. He could see the speculation and the disappointment in her eyes. "Why?"

"You don't think we should go on this mission, either," Anakin said.

"I voted to go." Marit's voice was firm. "The group rules."

"But I'm part of the group! The rule is that all decisions must be unanimous. Why isn't Rolai letting me vote?"

Marit shifted from one foot to the other. "He says new members shouldn't have full voting privileges until they've completed a mission —"

"And did you vote on that, or did Rolai just tell you?"

Marit's silence told him what he needed to know.

"So I'm supposed to risk my life without having a say in what we do? Do you think that's fair?"

"Do you think it's fair to sabotage our engines to get what you want?" Marit's voice rose challengingly. "How could you do this? I trusted you! I brought you into the group!"

Marit's brown eyes held anger and reproach. Anakin felt it was time for the truth. He owed her that.

"I'm a Jedi," he said. "I'm not really a student at the Leadership School. I was sent there to investigate Gillam Tarturi's disappearance."

"Gillam?" Marit was surprised.

"Don't you want to know what happened to him?" Anakin asked. "And before we left, Ferus Olin disappeared. What if Rolai had something to do with it? What if he's funding the squad with ransom money? He's the one in charge of your treasury, and he's the security expert. He's the one with the connection to Rana Halion. What if she got him to kidnap Gillam? All the pieces fit. Why did he lie to you about this mission? Don't you want to get to the bottom of it?"

Marit looked sad. "I wish you'd told me."

"I'm telling you now."

"You don't understand anything. Gillam —" Marit hesitated.

"So tell me," Anakin said, exasperated. "What about Gillam?"

"What about Gillam?" A mocking voice suddenly came from behind him.

Anakin whirled around. Gillam Tarturi stood, leaning against the wing of a starfighter. He was the same height as Anakin, and their eyes met across the space. Anakin felt shock and dismay ripple through him.

Anakin looked back at Marit. She nodded slowly.

"Gillam *is* the squad," she said. "It was his idea. He formed it. He made up the bylaws. He recruited us. We wouldn't have done anything without him. We would have been a bunch of miserable outcasts."

"You faked your disappearance," Anakin said to Gillam. "Why?"

"I have my reasons," Gillam replied lightly.

Marit spoke into her comlink. "We need you," she said crisply.

"What's going on?" Anakin asked.

For his answer, he heard the soft sound of her blaster leaving its holster. He could have stopped her easily, but he didn't. Marit pointed the blaster at him, a reluctant look on her face. Within seconds, the rest of the squad rushed into the hangar. Their blasters were drawn. They were all pointed at Anakin.

"I'm sorry," Marit said.

CHAPTER FIFTEEN

Marit's gaze was sorrowful. Rolai and Gillam looked hardened with purpose. But the others — Hurana, Tulah, and Ze — looked afraid. Why were they afraid? Anakin sensed that there was a conspiracy here. Gillam and Rolai were together, and they had roped in the rest of the reluctant squad. Except for Marit.

There is something going on here that even Marit doesn't know.

"He disabled the laser cannons on two of the starfighters," Marit told the others. "It's all right — I know how to fix it." She turned to Anakin. "We're going to have to restrain you until we're safely away."

Anakin looked at Gillam. "Is that so, Gillam? Why don't you tell her what you really have in mind?"

"Sorry, Marit," Gillam said easily. "That's not quite the plan."

"What's the plan, Gillam?" Anakin asked.

Marit gave Gillam a questioning look.

"How would the kidnapping disgrace Senator Tarturi if he wasn't implicated in something terrible?" Gillam said to Marit.

"And we get a very large bonus from Rana Halion, too," Rolai said.

"Think about what it will do for the countermovement, Marit," Gillam said. "The Senator kidnaps his own son to throw suspicion on the Ierians. And then something goes wrong, and his son dies —"

"And it's his fault," Rolai chortled. "He sacrificed his own son so he could keep his power!"

"I don't get it," Marit said.

"I do," Anakin said. "They want to kill me."

Shocked, Marit looked from Gillam to Rolai. "That can't be true."

"Actually, we were going to hand you over to Rana Halion for that particular step," Gillam said. "But as long as you pushed the issue . . ." He flourished his blaster and smiled at Anakin.

"But you're not Gillam — they'll figure that out," Marit said.

"They have a plan to disguise the body somehow," Anakin said. "I'm sure Rana Halion can find ways. I'll be taken for Gillam. And Senator Tarturi will not only be disgraced among his own people, he'll have a war on his hands. He won't be able to investigate, even if he wants to."

"Which he won't, because he won't care," Gillam said. "He'll just care about his Senatorial privileges being threatened."

"It's a brilliant plan," Rolai said.

Marit stared at the two of them. "You're both insane."

Gillam shook his head sadly. "Poor Marit. You lost your nerve on Tierell. That's why we couldn't trust you."

Marit looked at Tulah, Hurana, and Ze. "Are you going along with this?"

The three of them looked uncomfortable.

"Gillam says we must be warriors," Hurana said. "This is the only way."

"I just do the tech stuff," Ze said.

"This has nothing to do with me," Tulah said.

"Ah, one thing I should point out," Gillam said. "Because of the disappearance of another student, the school has gone into security code green. And that means that all passes have been cancelled. You've missed three of the hour check-ins."

"I knew I should have extended the range on our comlinks," Ze muttered.

"Which means we've been expelled," Hurana said.

"Which means, dear friends, that we have nowhere to go," Gillam said. "It's a big galaxy out there. We only have one another. And that's a *good* thing. Together, we can be the best. We can have everything we want, if we just stick together. At first we did it because nobody wanted us. But now we can do it because we're the best. We belong together."

Gillam's voice was low and compelling. Anakin saw the charisma and charm that had led these students to join him.

"Maybe nobody wanted the others," Anakin said. "Or you convinced them that it was true. I don't know about that. But what about you? You're the son of a powerful Senator. Who didn't want you?"

Gillam's face went white with sudden rage, and for the first time, Anakin could see that he was quite capable of killing him. "My father!" he shouted. Gillam regained control of himself with an effort. "And now he'll realize how wrong he was. Everyone will realize who underestimated my resolve. Well, Marit? Are you with us?"

Marit turned to Anakin. "I have nowhere else to go," she said.

"Marit, we're not doing anything wrong," Gillam said. "We're doing what we set out to do. We knew what the stakes were."

Anakin held Marit's gaze. "Did you know the stakes would be murder?"

"No one is asking you," Gillam snapped at Anakin. "You're already dead."

"He's a Jedi," Marit said. "If you think your plan will be easy, think again."

Gillam shrugged, coming closer to Anakin. "He has six blasters pointed at him. Even if you don't fire, I don't think we'll have a problem. I know the Jedi. I've seen them around the Senate all my life. They are basically servants of the Senators. Whatever power they had is gone now."

Anger coursed through Anakin. He saw the privilege Gillam had been brought up with, and how it had corrupted him. He saw that Gillam had counted on the feelings of the others, how they had felt lost and alone in a world he knew and they didn't. He had taken their minds and hearts and fashioned them into a weapon aimed at his father. The squad wasn't about justice. It was about revenge.

Anakin jumped up and kicked out with one foot in a spinning arc, booting the blaster from Gillam's hand while he held out a hand and, using the Force, tore Rolai's blaster from his grip. He landed on one leg and used the other to disarm Tulah with another well-aimed kick, grabbing the blaster from Ze's hand at the same time. He used his knee to dislodge the weapon from a surprised Hurana and then simply took Marit's from her hand. The entire series of attack moves took only seconds. The squad barely had time to blink.

Now they stared at him, or down at their empty hands. There was a beat, a moment of silence and surprise. Anakin pulled out and ignited his lightsaber, holding it in a posture any Jedi would recognize as offensive. He was ready to strike. He did not want to hurt anyone. That was his first concern. But he had to stop the squad's mission.

"Just don't move," he told them.

Anakin sensed movement behind him and turned slightly. Rana Halion had taken a step inside the hangar. As soon as she saw the lightsaber, she hit a button on her cuff.

Gillam smiled. "Looks like your luck has run out, Jedi."

"Jedi don't need luck," Anakin said, just as the attack droids swarmed into the hangar.

Blaster fire erupted from the droids, aimed at Anakin but scattered enough so that he feared for Marit and the others. The squad dropped, scrambling for their blasters. Anakin saw at once his problems. Gillam and Rolai had found blasters and were trying to aim at him as he moved. Fire from the droids was heavy. Marit had ducked behind a starfighter. He did not think he could count on help from her. She seemed dazed.

He saw the smile of triumph on Gillam's face as he retrieved and aimed his blaster, and Anakin's anger returned. He reached out to the Force. He remembered the lessons he had learned from Soara Antana, the great Jedi Master. *The Force comes from stillness*, she had said. *Find your still center, even in the midst of battle.*

He saw time unspool before him like a ribbon. He saw it freeze like ice on a river. He saw that he had infinite time to do everything he needed.

With an outstretched hand he knocked the blaster from Gillam's grasp and sent it flying across the full space of the hangar. It hit the wall so hard it shattered. Gillam's smile disappeared.

At the same time he was moving, diverting the droids' blaster fire from where Tulah and Hurana had taken cover, pushing Ze behind a durasteel container, and knocking out one attack droid with a thrust to its control panel.

Suddenly the laser cannons from the starfighter on his right began to fire. Gillam had slipped inside the cockpit.

Anakin did not lose his sense of frozen time. He was the master of time. He did not worry about the laser cannons any more than he'd worried about the attack droids. It all seemed so easy. He seemed to see the fire before it came, and he knew how to move to avoid it. His movements were like shimmersilk, so fluid it was as though he did not have muscles and bones, only will.

Now his Master was here. He could feel that, too. But he did not need him.

He spun in midair, taking out two battle droids while he leaped through the laser cannonfire straight at the cockpit of the starfighter. With one backward slash he took out the final droid. He had a flash of Gillam's shocked face as he cut through the windscreen with one slice. With one hand, he threw Gillam out of the pilot's seat and then dropped into it. He turned off the engines and disabled the laser cannons.

Siri and Ferus stood, lightsabers drawn, guarding Rolai, Marit, Hurana, Tulah, and Ze. Obi-Wan had captured Rana Halion.

Across the space, he looked at his Master. He

waited for Obi-Wan to acknowledge him. The mission was over. He had been successful. He had found Gillam and thwarted an invasion.

He waited, standing in the cockpit, looking down. He could feel the flush of triumph on his cheeks. Siri glanced at him, as did Ferus. He could see the astonishment on their faces. But his Master never looked up.

CHAPTER SIXTEEN

Never had Obi-Wan seen such a display of the Force from a Padawan. From the great Jedi Masters, yes. From Qui-Gon, near the end of his life. But from someone so young? Anakin's power astonished him. He had glimpsed it before, but now he had seen it unfurl, and it staggered him.

He had not had a chance to move, to help. Anakin had been a blur. He had seemed to be everywhere at once. He had destroyed ten attack droids, disarmed his aggressors, and disabled two laser cannons without hesitation, with even a slight smile on his face.

He could see that Siri and Ferus had been just as astonished at Anakin's deep connection to the Force, the way he had seemed to know what was going to happen before it happened, the way he was able to dodge fire before it occurred. Astonished, yes — and disturbed.

Unease settled into Obi-Wan's bones, joining his disappointment and the anger he had tried to eliminate from his heart. To have a Padawan so gifted who was capable of being so wrong — it was his gift to be able to teach him. It was his burden as well.

At first he could not even look at Anakin. He had to concentrate on the matter at hand.

Rana Halion tried to glide away from him, but with a lifted lightsaber he stopped her. "How dare you!" she cried. "I assure you, I have no idea what this renegade band is doing here. My security team alerted me that there was a break-in and I arrived to see a battle." Her eyes swept the secret squad as if she had never seen them before.

"And why did you send in droids to attack a Jedi?" Siri asked.

"How ridiculous. I didn't know there was a Jedi here," Rana Halion said. "We sent in the droids because it is the usual procedure when there is a security breach."

The girl called Marit raised her chin and fixed Rana with a contemptuous stare. "She is lying," she said. "About everything. I'm not a student anymore, but I can see I've learned my first real lesson today. Betrayals are the way the galaxy works." She looked at Anakin.

He shook his head at her, as if to apologize. "I believed in what you believed," he said.

"Then you were as foolish as I was," Marit said softly.

"You'll take her word over mine?" Rana Halion huffed.

"This is a matter for the Senate to sort out," Siri said. "These students will testify, no doubt. They've already been expelled, so they'll certainly be available."

"Expelled? I don't think so," Gillam said. "I want to talk to my father!"

"Your father might not want to talk to you after he discovers that you were trying to set him up for murder," Obi-Wan said.

"Who told such lies?" Gillam asked. "I barely escaped my captors with my life. She kidnapped me!" he shrilled, pointing at Rana Halion.

"You scrawny brat!" Rana cried.

Ferus held up Gillam's datapad. "You might want to reconsider what you're saying, Gillam. Do you recognize this?"

Gillam went pale, but only for a moment. "I don't know what he's talking about. I don't even know him.

I've never seen that datapad. He's just another jealous student, no doubt."

"No, he is a Jedi," Siri said.

Gillam looked alarmed. "He's a Jedi, too?"

"They're everywhere," Tulah said, dazed.

"I never realized how much you lie," Marit said to Gillam. "You breathe, you lie. This squad was never about us. It wasn't about banding together to do something good. It was really all about you. And if you think the rest of us are going to support your lies, you're not only a liar, you're crazy. Like you said, Gillam, we all have nothing left to lose."

"Affirmatively true," Ze said, and Tulah nodded.

Gillam looked flustered. He opened his mouth and then clamped it shut. He crossed his arms. "I want to see my father," he repeated.

"You'll see him soon enough," Siri said. "We're taking you all to Coruscant. The Senate authorities can straighten out this mess."

Siri led a protesting Rana Halion away. Ferus herded the squad toward the open doors of the hangar.

Obi-Wan was left alone with Anakin. At last it was time for him to speak to his Padawan. Yet he could not find the right words. He knew, glancing at his Padawan's eager face, that Anakin meant well from the bottom of his heart. If Obi-Wan saw a shadow on that heart, he knew it would pain his Padawan to know it. In many ways, Anakin was still a boy. A wounded, loving, anxious boy with great gifts he did not fully understand.

Yet he was also a young man, close to maturity, who could do great harm. To others, yes. To himself, most of all.

"They were going to conduct a raid on Andara," Anakin said, tired of Obi-Wan's silence. "But first they were going to kill me —"

"I know," Obi-Wan said. "Everything was on Gillam's datapad. Which you would have known if you had searched for Ferus."

Anakin flushed. "I didn't know where he was."

"You did not look."

"I thought perhaps he was on Ieria or Andara. I thought the secret squad knew where he was —"

"You did not even *look*!" Obi-Wan shouted. "Your fellow Jedi was missing, and you did not even look!"

"I thought it best to continue under cover," Anakin said. His face showed his surprise at Obi-Wan's harshness. Obi-Wan never raised his voice. "I had infiltrated the squad. I thought my best chance of finding both Gillam and Ferus was to continue."

"You were willing to participate in a raid that would

have started a war," Obi-Wan continued. He had to struggle to keep his voice level. He needed to keep as calm as possible.

"I didn't know about the raid!" Anakin protested. "I mean, I knew they were going to do something, but it was a dry run, designed to show the Andarans that they had the capability of invading their airspace. I didn't know they had plans to destroy their fleet. As soon as I did, I sabotaged the laser cannons."

"Anakin, you left your fellow Jedi imprisoned and went off on a mission with a group of beings who you had no reason to trust," Obi-Wan said. "You were wrong at every point. Can't you see that?"

Anakin said nothing.

"You did not contact me to tell me Ferus was missing —"

"I would have compromised our cover —"

"You had a responsibility!" Obi-Wan's voice cut like a laser whip. "Just as I had one to Siri. You betrayed me and the Order by your actions. And your inability to see that troubles me the worst of all."

"I am sorry, Master."

Obi-Wan shook his head. Grief rose in him. "Those are words you speak so easily, Padawan."

Anakin's mouth closed in a line. "I don't know what you want from me."

Honesty. Loyalty. Patience. Obedience. Obi-Wan thought these things but did not say them. Because, after all, they were only words, too.

"I can only show you the path," Obi-Wan said. "You must choose to walk on it."

"I just . . ." Anakin stopped. He took a ragged breath. "I thought you would be proud of me."

I am proud of you. Obi-Wan wanted to say the words. They were true. He was proud of so much in Anakin. But now was not the time to tell him that.

Or was it?

Help me, Qui-Gon.

But no matter how hard Obi-Wan listened, he could not hear the quiet wisdom of his Master. And now it was too late. Siri returned and signaled to him. It was time to go.

"I will take this matter up with the Council," he said.

"Of course," Anakin said. "The Council. We can't take a step without it."

"That's enough!" Obi-Wan snapped. "Come. The others are waiting."

Anakin hesitated. The set of his mouth was stubborn.

"Come, Padawan." Obi-Wan's tone rang with authority. Anakin's hesitation cast a chill on his heart.

Anakin followed him. Obi-Wan did not glance back again.

He felt shaken. Did Anakin understand that he had violated an essential part of the Jedi code? Did he know he had broken something between them? He had not fully trusted Obi-Wan. And so Obi-Wan had lost his trust in him.

Not for good, he tried to reassure himself. *And maybe not for long.*

Still, his step was heavy as he climbed up the loading ramp of the transport. His anger faded. Left behind was a feeling he was not used to experiencing. It was fear.